A
STITCH
IN TIME

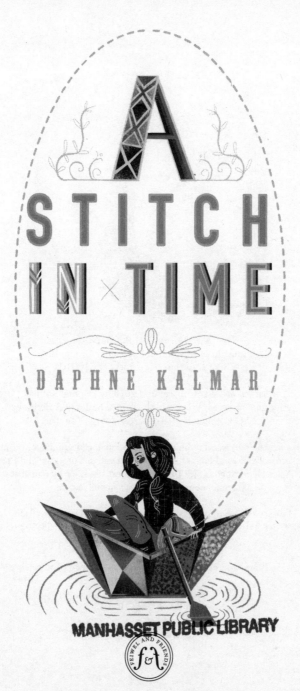

A STITCH IN × TIME

DAPHNE KALMAR

FEIWEL AND FRIENDS • NEW YORK

A FEIWEL AND FRIENDS BOOK
An imprint of Macmillan Publishing Group, LLC
175 Fifth Avenue, New York, NY 10010

Our books may be purchased in bulk for promotional, educational, or business use.
Please contact your local bookseller or the Macmillan Corporate and Premium
Sales Department at (800) 221-7945 ext. 5442 or by e-mail at
MacmillanSpecialMarkets@macmillan.com.

Library of Congress Cataloging-in-Publication Data is available.
ISBN 978-1-250-15498-9 (hardcover) / ISBN 978-1-250-15497-2 (ebook)

Book design by Rebecca Syracuse
Feiwel and Friends logo designed by Filomena Tuosto
First edition, 2018

1 3 5 7 9 10 8 6 4 2

mackids.com

For Georg con cariño

1

In her nightclothes in the early morning light, Donut perched on the chair at the small desk in her room. She held a number sixteen glass eye with a clamp, lining up the iris so it looked forward and to the right. Once before she had so concentrated on the socket and the wood glue drying that she had popped the eyeball in backward. There was no fixing it. That little deer mouse would forever gaze into the pitch-black of its own empty skull.

It wasn't so much the mice and birds themselves that fascinated Donut. It was the precise steps needed to put them back together. Sam had taught her how to prepare the skins and stitch them up all perfect, stuffed with cotton batting, dusted with arsenic powder to kill the lice and other vermin. It was making them almost as good as new that gave her the patience to undertake the tiny stitches with linen thread and curved needle.

Donut could hear Aunt Agnes downstairs clanking the door to the woodstove, filling the teakettle. Since her aunt had arrived three weeks ago, she'd been arguing with the old stove—loading the firebox with too much wood, burning the bread and biscuits. "Like cooking in the Dark Ages," she grumbled.

Donut slipped the glass eye into the left socket.

"There you go," she whispered.

She kept her taxidermy private, stowed away in her mother's cedar hope chest. Three voles, eleven mice, two chickadees, three house wrens, a cardinal, and a bluebird—practice specimens. The mice and voles came from traps that mostly broke their necks. Her best friend, Tiny, brought her the birds, offerings from Bangor, his Maine coon cat, who left them on the rag rug right inside his kitchen door.

Aunt Agnes didn't approve and Donut suspected that her mother, whose delicate porcelain knickknacks lined the shelves in the parlor, would not have allowed the chemicals, skins, scalpels, and such. But then, Donut and her mother had crossed paths just the once, on the day Donut was born, the same day her mother died. Her mother, Rose, probably would not have approved of Donut's nickname, either. Dorothy was the name she'd picked out. Pops said that if the baby was a girl, Rose had wanted her to have a proper name, three syllables, unlike her own. But the name Dorothy had faded away without her mother there to protect it. And then there was the colic.

Her pops couldn't abide baby Dorothy's fussing and crying due to the colic and discovered that one of Mrs. Lamphere's maple-cream donuts always did the trick. Gumming at the sweet frosting sent her right to sleep. That probably explained why she had no fear of rodents, as her crib often had visitors late at night—field mice, deer mice, gathering crumbs and bits of icing twisted up in the blanket. Her pops had told her of the scampering, the sprinkling of tiny black mouse droppings that he shook out of the bedding every morning.

Aunt Agnes would have keeled over in fright at the thought of all the small mammals visiting Donut as a baby, like furry fairies. The thought made her smile as she inserted the second eye.

Donut examined her work. The mouse's body was so light in her left palm. Without the feel of the scrambling feet, the sharp toenails digging in, there was nothing left. What was it like to be dead, stuffed and preserved by an eleven-year-old girl, eyeballs and guts gone, empty like the seashell on the windowsill whispering the sound of the ocean up against her ear?

"Where are you, mouse?" she said, sitting very still. There was no answer.

Donut wrapped up the mouse in a square of red flannel

and stowed it in her mother's chest. She pulled on her pants and a wool shirt. Not bothering with a brush, she braided her long brown hair. With a tight fist she tapped her *Rand McNally World Atlas*, second edition, three times for luck.

Her pops had said that a big part of geography was rivers. Towns and cities grew up along waterways like pearls on a necklace, so she'd decided to organize her study of geography river by river. She'd finished the Nile, and now she was learning the names of towns and cities strung along the Mississippi.

"New Orleans, Baton Rouge." Donut reeled them off. "Vidalia, Arkansas City, Helena, Memphis, St. Louis, Hannibal, Keokuk, Davenport, Dubuque, La Crosse, St. Paul, Minneapolis, Bemidji. Got it."

It was Saturday—launch day. Pops had designed and built his boat at Mr. Daniels' factory, where he'd worked. Newfangled furnaces, manure spreaders, and milk coolers were their business, but her pops had big dreams for his little boat. They'd been waiting for the spring, for the ice on Dog Pond to melt.

"You and me, Donut," he'd said, "in the footsteps of Henry Hudson, Lewis and Clark, the Wright Brothers, Ernest Shackleton. We'll launch my folding boat and make history or get very wet trying." He'd laughed at the thought of it.

"Ready-made shipwreck," Mr. Daniels said. "I told him it'd never sell. A surefire drowning bucket."

Well, she and Tiny were going to prove him wrong.

Donut stuck a pencil behind her ear and grabbed her canvas book bag. Taking two steps at a time, she ran down the stairs.

The kitchen was warm and smelled of toast. Aunt Agnes sat at the table wearing a dress so full of flowers, so pink and purple, it was looking for a fight. She stirred her tea with a rapid-fire clinking. One of her thick books lay open by her plate—not one adventure story or mystery or interesting fact hiding in the whole blasted thing. Aunt Agnes's head should have exploded by now from the boredom.

"Good morning. Oatmeal's hot on the stove. We need to have a little chat, so just slow yourself down." Aunt Agnes took a slurp of tea and smiled. "I opened up a can of peaches for a special treat."

Peaches? A chat? What was going on? Aunt Agnes was all love and kisses like Earle Barclay on slaughtering day. He'd scratch a hog's back with a rake until it was twitching with happiness, pick up his shotgun, and shoot it dead.

"No time for chatting. Gotta get my chores done and meet Tiny."

"Well, you'll just have to make time." Aunt Agnes picked her napkin up off the table and gave it a good snap. Terrified crumbs flew in all directions. Pasting a smile back on her face she said, "Get your breakfast. You'll be steadier with food in you."

"I'll be right back." Donut turned and headed for the mudroom. She had to get some air, get away from her auntie's smile. And the chat didn't sound too promising, either. Besides, she needed the paddles for the launch.

"Where are you going?" called Aunt Agnes.

Donut didn't answer. She got her boots and coat on and slipped outside. The storage shed by the woodpile was packed with the hardware, engine parts, and odds and ends her pops had collected. During the New Year's Day blizzard he'd dug a path out there just to get his hands on a sheet of tin and a rusty box of old bike gears for one of his inventions.

The paddles were there. She'd spotted them ages ago, way in the back. Donut stood in the yard, not moving. The shed had been closed up tight since the accident. Since her pops had died. Maybe it was a mistake to open the door. A piece of him that was stored up inside would float up into the clouds. The wind would grab hold and carry him away from the green hills of Vermont and out over the stormy North Atlantic Ocean.

Donut couldn't stay still with the thought of the wind and the open ocean and her pops, but she couldn't move any closer to the shed, either. The cold night had capped the puddles on the dirt drive with a thin skim of ice. Donut reached out her foot to the nearest puddle and cracked the ice with the toe of her boot. She lifted her other foot and stomped on the next puddle, shattering the ice. She kept going, reeling off her Mississippi towns. "New Orleans," stomp. "Baton Rouge," stomp. "Vidalia," stomp. "Arkansas City, Helena, Memphis, St. Louis," stomp, stomp, stomp, stomp. Muddy water oozed up over the broken shards.

Donut eyed the shed. "Enough. Just put a penny in it. Get going."

Donut marched past the woodpile, right up close to the shed, and paused. For just an instant she believed, really believed, that she'd find her pops in there, rummaging around, wearing his lucky shirt—red flannel with a burn hole in the left sleeve. He'd turn, smile, and wink.

Her guts twisted up tight.

With both hands Donut yanked the door open.

The air inside was old and musty. The shelves along the walls were packed with crates and glass jars. Wire, sheet metal, and boards were stacked on the floor. Donut swung her arms in front of her face to hack through the spider-webs and picked her way into the far corner, where she could make out the paddles.

Carrying them under one arm, she backed out of the shed and shoved the door shut. Her pops' treasures were just junk now. No one would see the wheel spokes and umbrella handles, the hooks and pulleys the same as he had. "Got po-tential," he'd say. The weight of it slowed her down. Every day she kept losing pieces of him. His old shed would dis-appear, too. Over time, rain and melted snow would seep through the cracks. Shingles would come loose, nails would rust out. The whole kit and caboodle would fall into a rotted, rusted heap, like Mr. Hollis's old barn on Kate Brook Road.

Donut leaned the paddles against the woodpile. Inside the mudroom she pulled in a deep breath, then yanked off her coat and hung it on a peg.

"Dorothy?" called Aunt Agnes. "What are you up to?"

"Nothing." Donut kicked off her boots. "Nothing, noth-ing, nothing," she mumbled.

In the kitchen Donut spooned a dollop of oatmeal into a bowl and passed on the canned peaches just to spite Aunt Agnes. She didn't like oatmeal, but her auntie was convinced that children, like horses, should have a dose of oats every day. Donut and her pops had cooked up eggs and some of Mr. Barclay's sausages most mornings. Tiny usually showed up for a second breakfast after he and his dad were done with the morning milking. He never came now, what with the oatmeal and Aunt Agnes sitting at the table.

Donut sat across from her auntie and poured some cream from the jug into her bowl along with a good measure of maple syrup.

"You'll have your Saturday soon enough," said Aunt Agnes. "But we must talk. It's been three weeks now since your father's passing. Your Aunt Jo and I are agreed that it's time to think about your future."

Donut clenched her fists under the table. Aunt Agnes had arrived the day of the funeral, wearing a black hat and shiny black dress, acting like an old crow perched on a branch, bossing and squawking. That very afternoon, while Donut hid out at Sam's, her auntie had dragged empty suitcases and two old trunks up from the cellar into Pops' bedroom. She'd packed up all his clothes, his shoes, his hats, his coats, cleared off his chest of drawers and bedside table. After she finished she'd moved right in—hanging up her dresses in his closet, laying out her brush and comb and hairpins by the washbowl where his pipe and pocketknife and razor used to be. Her pops had only just been buried, and Aunt Agnes had wasted no time in clearing all that was left of him out of his own house. Donut took hold of the table edge, studied her fingers as they went all white and pink. She gave her aunt a good long look.

"You and Aunt Jo ought to keep your hands off my future. It's mine."

Aunt Agnes stiffened. "Young lady, that's just the kind of behavior Jo and I are concerned about. You are at the cusp of womanhood. Here it is 1927, the modern age, and you are behaving like a young barbarian."

Aunt Agnes took a chomp of toast slathered in store-bought jam. There was no escaping her. And Donut knew she had to keep quiet or her auntie would cancel Saturday altogether, and Pops' boat was waiting. Tiny would be waiting down at Sam's.

Donut stared at the lump of gray oatmeal nicely centered on her mother's fine bone china. Purple pansies ran around the rim. The blob, surrounded by cream and syrup, was shaped like Australia, with a raisin on the east coast marking Sydney Harbor. She would raise the sails on her ship, skim across the creamy sea, head south to Tasmania, or east to New Zealand. Make friends with marsupials as they lapped up the blobs of maple syrup washing ashore.

"Are you even listening to me?" said Aunt Agnes, fussing with her napkin.

"Yes, Auntie." Donut built up the Australian Alps with the back of her spoon.

"That's an improvement. Now, finish your breakfast so we can have a proper conversation. I'll be in the parlor."

Donut ate as much of the oatmeal as she could

stomach. The peaches would have helped. She cleared her dishes and scraped what was left of Australia into the slop bucket.

"Dorothy?"

"Yes, Auntie."

Donut stopped at the parlor door. Aunt Agnes sat in her mother's wingback chair knitting another sock, working her way through a ball of gray yarn. All she ever knitted was socks. Gray or black. When she had a dozen pairs or so, she'd ship them down to the Soldiers' Home. Donut figured the home was full of old men shuffling around in those socks, polishing up the floors, slipping once in a while and breaking an arm or a leg, their war medals pinned on their chests clinking together as they landed.

Aunt Agnes peered at Donut over her reading glasses. "Sit down. I'll just finish this row."

The click-clack of the bone needles started up again. Donut sat, gripped the seat of her chair, stared at the fire in the fireplace. Her house was emptied of all the familiar Saturday sounds—her pops whistling, the dings and clanks of his tinkering at the kitchen table. She'd sit across from him, the *Rand McNally World Atlas*, second edition, opened up to the African continent. They'd lose track of time; eat a whole sack of Mrs. Lamphere's gingersnaps for lunch.

"What would you want to see most of all?" she'd ask.

"Panama Canal," he'd say. "And you?"

"Elephants."

The click-clack of the knitting needles stopped and Donut looked up. Aunt Agnes set her knitting down on the side table, laid her hands flat on the arms of the chair, and smiled. "Dorothy, I'll come right to the point. Your aunt Jo and I have decided it's time for you to come live with us in Boston. It's what—"

"Boston!" Donut stood, her legs kicking the chair over backward. "I'm not moving to Boston."

She stared at her aunt, stared hard and clenched her teeth so tight her head hurt. Aunt Agnes pursed her lips and stared right back, then she smiled again. Smiled.

"It's a shock, I know," she said. "We'll be leaving in two weeks. On April thirtieth. You'll settle right in at the academy. Free tuition with my position as administrator and your aunt Jo as headmistress. We'll be all together."

"Two weeks! Together? Who said I wanted any part of together? Me, at a stuffy girls' school, living with a couple of bent hairpins who—"

"Dorothy, control yourself." Aunt Agnes's voice had an edge to it that would scare the birds right out of the trees. "You do not have a choice in the matter. Now pick up that chair and sit down."

She didn't pick the chair up. She didn't sit down. "You'll have to tie me up, stuff me in a sack, and carry me out of here. I'm not going."

Donut kicked the fallen chair out of her way, stomped into the mudroom, and pulled on her boots and coat.

"Don't you dare leave this house," said Aunt Agnes from the parlor.

Donut grabbed her book bag, slammed the front door behind her, and ran. At the road she slowed to a walk. With each step she kicked a rock into the scrub. She kicked those rocks so hard they'd kill a cat.

Boston.

She'd been to Boston once with her pops. They'd taken the train and spent the night in a hotel that was four stories tall. Even that high up, close to the low-hanging clouds, there was such a racket floating up from below she hardly slept a wink. In the streets there wasn't room to move, what with the automobiles, horses, and wagons hauling milk, coal, or ice, peddlers with pushcarts, telegraph boys flying by on bicycles, and more people than she could count. That was the one and only time she'd ever met them—Aunt Jo and Aunt Agnes in their sitting room in Boston, firing off questions while Donut and her pops squirmed, all stiff and awkward in their city clothes.

Donut turned and glared at her house, all filled up with this aunt, her mother's sister, someone she barely knew.

"I won't go, you old bat. Just try to make me."

Donut twirled around and stormed down the hill.

Sam would know what to do.

3

Donut pushed Sam's front door open with her shoulder. In the mudroom she dodged books, collecting jars, nets, and crates. Countless stuffed birds stared down at her from shelves and racks. A pair of blue jays, finches, woodpeckers, a sharp-eyed raven, all of them watched her as she rushed through the room.

Tiny, Sam, and a gigantic moose, or at least what was left of it, filled the parlor. Tiny, in his overalls and stocking feet, taking up more space than any twelve-year-old had a right to, held a rope running through a pulley bolted to the ceiling. The other end of the rope supported the part skeleton, part wire, part wooden body of a headless moose hanging in a cat's cradle of knots and loops. Sam, gray hair sticking out in odd places, his glasses falling down his nose, was lying on the floor with a wrench in one hand while he tugged at the left rear leg rod with the other.

"She's gonna haul me off to Boston," said Donut, looking from Sam to Tiny.

"Your aunt? What do you mean?" said Tiny. He relaxed his grip on the rope, the pulley squeaked, and the moose sagged a few inches.

"Up. Up. Hold it steady," said Sam. He rolled over and eyed Donut. "Can this wait? We're right in the middle—"

"No. You don't understand. It's for good. Forever."

Donut stood there in the parlor, glaring at the two of them, the muddy wet of her boots making puddles on the floor. What was wrong with them? Dumb moose wasn't going anywhere.

"Forever?" said Tiny, straining on the rope with both hands above his head.

"Aunt Agnes and Aunt Jo, they want to move me to Boston. In two weeks. For good. And I'm not going."

Sam set his wrench down and sat up. He scratched at his ear.

The pulley squealed, the moose sagged, and he turned away.

"This is difficult news," said Sam over his shoulder. "And I don't want to put you off, but it's a delicate moment. Weeks of work to get to this point."

"Boston. That's a long ways away." Tiny shook his head.

"Miles and miles," said Donut.

"Just hold the femur, would you?" said Sam.

The only way to grab Sam's full attention was to get this blasted moose standing on his own four feet. Donut kneeled down on the floor and got hold of the leg bone with both hands. Sam picked up the wrench and tugged at the iron rod, trying to slip it into the hole he'd drilled in the spruce slab that was propped up on blocks.

"Can your aunties really do that?" said Tiny. Donut could only see his legs from underneath the moose.

"They're Donut's legal guardians now, I'm afraid," said Sam. "Lower it just a tad. Good." He slipped the rod into the hole and lay down on his back with the wrench.

Donut moved around Sam to the back end of the moose and nudged and pushed the right leg rod.

"Easy there. Gentle pressure," he said.

Donut scowled at the back of his head and looked up at Tiny, who winked. She had half a mind to cut the rope.

"Sam, Pops made you my godfather. Doesn't that give you a say?"

"Your pops named Agnes as your godmother, so it's pretty much a standoff. But none of that matters. It's in his will—if anything was to happen to him, your aunts would be your guardians."

"But he didn't say they could kidnap me, did he?"

Sam didn't answer.

"Yeah," said Tiny. "They can't kidnap her."

The last leg took forever—there was no give anywhere. Finally, Donut jammed it through. Sam, wheezing a little now, secured the last nut and clambered up off the floor.

Tiny, who was a head taller than Sam, untied the tangle of rope. The moose was very unmoose-like, almost dainty. It stood on tiptoe, six inches of bare iron holding up the leg bones all wired up to the body board. A moose ballerina until Sam attached the four enormous hoofs waiting on the workbench.

"Good to have the old boy standing," said Sam.

"I'm not going," said Donut.

Sam leaned down and picked up his wrench. "I know this is very difficult. But I suppose your aunt wants to go home. Not many job prospects here, either."

"Let her go home. I'm just fine where I am. I'll get myself a big dog and be loads happier."

"There's gotta be something she can do," said Tiny.

"I'm afraid not. The law is such that Donut has no say in the matter."

"That's just not right. What am I? A lamp or a chair she can cart around?" Donut kicked at the spruce slab, the moose rocked, and Sam cringed.

She walked over to his workbench, pulled herself up on one of the stools and shoved her hands in her coat pockets.

She'd put up with more than her fair share of rotten luck already, what with her mother dying before she'd even gotten a good look at her and then her pops, with the tire blowing out and the crash. Donut looked up. Sam was studying her with pinched-faced worry. Tiny was fingering one of his throwing rocks, looking for something to aim at.

"You might try gentle persuasion," said Sam. "She probably misses her sister."

"But what about me and my missing everything?" She was yelling now. "I never asked her to come here and take charge of me."

Tiny jammed the rock back in his pocket. Sam just shook his head.

She could see that even if he understood how wrong it was, Sam was gonna flop right down on Aunt Agnes's side. He had been her pops' best friend. She'd known him all her life. But he was still an adult who'd forgotten what it was like to be a kid, all tied up in rules and schedules and punishments with no say.

"Donut," he said, "that temper of yours will make things worse."

"I thought you'd be on my side."

"It's not about sides," he said.

"Says you."

"Donut."

She eyed Tiny. "I'll meet you up the hill." He nodded and she started toward the door.

"Donut," said Sam.

"Gotta go."

In the mudroom Donut paused, surrounded by the stuffed birds—Sam's flock, as he called them. When she was little, she'd lie down on her back in this room and talk to each one. Now, as always, they were perched in watchful silence. Time was stopped—all stitched up with needle and thread. The birds were fixed in their spots on the shelves and cabinets, earthbound. Donut wished deep down in her guts that today they'd decide to fly. She'd open the front door and they'd swoop out into the world in a rush of feathers and song.

"Donut," said Sam from the parlor door. "Stay awhile. Beryl made some stewed apples."

His soft voice nearly cracked her open like a walnut. Angry as a chained dog and so close to tears she could hardly breathe, all she could do was run. Donut blurted out a goodbye and got herself out the door and halfway up the hill before she slowed down. First Aunt Agnes, now Sam. She'd slammed the door on both of them, and the day had hardly started.

"Hey, wait up."

She turned. Tiny waved, his dad's cast-off red jacket slung over his shoulder. Donut pulled in a deep breath to steady herself.

"You okay?" he said, joining her.

"No."

"Is the launch still on?"

"Yeah."

"You sure about this?" he said, giving her a friendly punch on the arm, throwing her off-balance.

"Come on," she said. "Worst that could happen is it'll sink."

Tiny laughed. "No. Add to that the two of us drowning. That'll win the prize for worst."

Donut gave him a good punch. "Don't worry. She's seaworthy."

They grabbed the paddles by the woodpile at her house, Tiny pulled on his jacket, and they started up Slapp Hill Road. Donut had to do a bit of trotting every few yards to keep up with him.

"I'm not going to Boston," she said, panting a little.

Tiny leaned down and picked up a smooth stone. He pitched it at a maple tree and it pinged off the bark. "Of course you're not," he said.

And that was that.

With the cold air and the walking and Tiny beside her like always, side-arming rocks at maples and ash and poplars, Donut's stomach settled down. Her main worry right then was how wet they were going to get. Her pops' boat was a little thing, and Tiny was very big.

At the top of Slapp Hill, Donut and Tiny passed his house and the worn red barn. In the pasture alongside the road a herd of Guernseys grazed on the new grass, heads down, tails swinging.

One cow, ears twitching, followed them in the narrow, muddy track on her side of the barbed-wire fence.

"Hey, Winnie," called Donut.

Tiny jumped the gully, leaned over the fence, and gave her a scratch behind the ears.

Donut joined him and ran her hand down Winnie's soft brown neck.

"No apples today, girl," said Tiny.

Every one of the Patoines' Guernseys had a name, but Winnie had been raised up by Tiny, and she was his special favorite. When he was six years old his dad had trucked her to the Tunbridge Fair, and Tiny'd collected a blue ribbon for the finest heifer in the state. Winnie followed him around like a puppy—a very big puppy.

Tiny gave Winnie a friendly slap on the rump. "Go on, girl."

Despite his urging to join the herd, she followed them the length of the pasture and watched as they continued on down the road.

At the bottom of the hill they heard Ernie Mayo's flivver coming up behind them. The old Ford backfired, sputtered, and coughed. He didn't slow down as he approached, just held tight to the steering wheel with both hands, his police cap pulled down over his ears. They moved off to the side of the road and Ernie glared at them as he tore past.

"What's eating him?" said Donut.

"Probably thinks you got a bottle of hooch in your sack," said Tiny. "Thinks everyone and their granny's running whiskey out of Canada."

"If liquor was legal maybe he'd be a little friendlier."

"No," said Tiny. "My dad said Ernie was a cold fish long before Prohibition."

At the turnoff Tiny picked up a few more smooth stones and jammed them into his pocket. They left the road and headed along the footpath to the pond.

"Water's gonna be freezing. And even if your sardine can

floats, we don't know if it's gonna leak or not." Tiny whipped a stone into a stand of poplar trees.

"It was Pops' design. He built it. Won't be any leaks," said Donut. "We've just got to test how much weight it'll hold."

"So, I'm your sack of rocks?" Tiny laughed.

"Kinda." Donut grinned.

In the shadowy part of the trail she slowed down.

"I gotta think of something, Tiny. Can't live in a city, all bricked up, stuck in my aunties' school for curly heads in petticoats."

The thought of it stopped her altogether. She leaned her paddle against a cedar tree and sat down on a low boulder by the path. Tiny sat next to her.

"Your auntie's not been too bad up to now. My mom thinks she comes across as kinda snooty, but it's mostly all her book learning that puts people off. What's she thinking with you and Boston?"

Donut picked up a stick and busted it in two. "I don't give a fiddlehead what she's thinking. Just need to work up a plan. I've got almost five dollars from my poker winnings if I need it."

"That's money for your new atlas. You've been saving forever."

"The *Rand McNally World Atlas*, third edition, might just have to wait."

"What about getting her married off to Mr. Hollis or André? Get her down to one of the dances at the Grange Hall and introduce 'em. Then she'll have to stick around."

"Married? She's too old for that—pushing fifty. Besides, Mr. Hollis is ancient and André'd be scared to death of her." Donut stuffed her hands in her pockets. "We could take a shot at a little kidnapping, ourselves. We could get hold of something to make her sleep, like a bottle of chloroform or ether. You could help me pack her in a wooden crate. We'd put some straw in first, steal Sam's truck, haul the crate down to the train depot."

"Now, that's an excellent plan, excepting I'm not stealing a truck and your auntie is a solidly built lady. We'd be hard put to move her without busting one of her legs or a hip."

Donut kicked at the soft soil at her feet. "We'd be sure to drug her in the parlor so we wouldn't have far to heft her. And it wouldn't be stealing, just borrowing the truck. We'd ship her off to South America. Buenos Aires, maybe. With my poker winnings, I've probably got enough for the postage. We'd pack her up with jam jars filled with water, canned salmon, and crackers. And she'd need a pot to pee in. We'd throw in her knitting to pass the time. She could knit those old socks in the dark. Waking up in the crate would surely send her round the bend. She'd forget her name, join a convent."

"She's gonna have to do more than take a whiz, what with the salmon and the crackers. Gonna smell like Lazy Leon's barn in August."

"Those South Americans are gonna get a shock when they open up that crate and find a ripe auntie inside."

They both laughed, sitting on the gray boulder in the woods, the damp earth smell and the greenness coming on strong in the spring air. Donut could almost imagine Aunt Agnes long gone. But instead she was just sitting in the parlor, probably writing one of her letters to Aunt Jo with all her happy news about dragging their niece south to the big city to scrub the rough patches off and civilize her right up.

"I'd rather run off and live in the woods than let her drag me to Boston," she said in a louder voice than she intended.

Tiny shook his head. "That wouldn't do much good unless you could hold out for years and years."

"Maybe she wouldn't wait that long." Donut stood, brushed the moss and leaves off her backside. "Let's get moving."

After about a quarter mile, the trees opened up and they came out on the rocky edge of Dog Pond. It was a big pond, a lake really, shaped like a kidney bean, with a few run-down cabins plunked down along the shore here and there. No one was on the water, it being so early in the spring, which made it seem all the bigger.

They pushed their way through the scrub to where they'd hidden the boat in a patch of wild raspberry canes. Two weeks ago they'd lugged the tin boat here all the way from Mr. Daniels' factory. Now, finally, a spell of warm weather had melted the last of the ice.

It was a flat-bottomed skiff about eight feet long, squared off on both ends. And it folded. That had been her pops' brilliant idea. Right across the middle he'd attached strips of oilcloth and cedar planks that latched down to make it watertight. Using the grab handles on each end Donut and Tiny hauled the boat down to the rocky shore. They opened it up like a clamshell, twisted the eight latches closed, and set the paddles inside.

"Kinda windy," said Tiny, shaking his head. "And cold. Perfect day for floating around in the *Tintanic*."

"It's not the *Tintanic*. And we're not gonna sink," said Donut.

Tiny sat on a rock and pulled off his boots and socks. "Don't know why I listen to you."

Donut grinned. "Don't worry. I got this all planned out."

5

Donut studied the waves moving across the pond. "We'll have to hold her with the rope tied to the front—that's called the bow, you know. The back's called the stern, and the rope's called the painter."

"What kind of name is that for a rope?"

"I got the correct seafaring lingo out of my *Encyclopedia Britannica*. They had a drawing with arrows."

"Thought a painter was some guy with a brush and a bucket, but what do I know?"

Donut pulled the rope out from under the stern bench seat and tied it to the handle on the squared-off bow. Now that they were all set for the launch, she wasn't feeling so confident. Maybe her pops had planned to make a few more adjustments to the oilcloth or the latches.

"Come on." Donut kicked a rock. "Let's get cracking."

"Aye, aye, Captain."

They muscled the boat sideways into the shallows. It made a racket on the stones. Donut cringed at the thought of punctures and the worry that she hadn't brought anything to bail water with if some of the pond happened to slip in. But the little tin boat bobbed up and down in the water in a cheerful way, all ready for passengers.

"Looks swell," said Tiny. "Just comes across awful delicate."

"Lightweight, not delicate," said Donut.

She pulled off her boots and socks and rolled up her pants.

"Hold the painter tight," said Donut. The rocks dug into her bare feet. She stepped into the icy water and gritted her teeth at the cold of it.

She'd been in a canoe with her pops, so she knew that getting in and out was the tricky part about boating. Donut held the side and stretched her right leg up, over, and in. The boat tipped, she pulled back a little, and the boat rocked. Thinking too hard on this was going to get her very wet. In one go Donut reached across and grabbed the far side of the boat as she hauled her left leg in. The boat rolled toward her and water sloshed over the side. Donut dropped onto the stern seat and squirmed around into a crouch. Any sudden move and it got to rocking again.

"So far, so good. A little touchy, though," said Tiny.

Donut pressed her bare feet against the flat bottom. "Okay, I'm ready for you."

Tiny didn't move. "It's as good as walking the plank, me climbing into this thing."

"It's not gonna sink."

Tiny just shook his head, stepped into the water, and got up alongside the boat. Donut gripped the sides. With Tiny right there, so darn big, it really didn't look like the boat would hold him.

"Don't second-guess yourself," she said. "Do it fast."

"Let me concentrate."

Donut bit her tongue and held her breath. Tiny reached across and grabbed the far edge, lifted his right leg, and plunked his foot on the bottom of the boat.

"Steady," he whispered. "Steady."

With Tiny halfway in the boat, it rocked like a bronco, and water sloshed over the side. He pulled his other leg up out of the pond and sat down heavily on the middle bench seat. His weight settled the tin boat right down, but it floated low in the water, low enough that an ambitious fish might jump right in.

"I don't know how I'm gonna get back out," said Tiny, shaking his head, taking one of the paddles from Donut. "But sinking's gonna solve that problem."

"We're at sea." Donut gazed out over Dog Pond, the

breeze kicking up little waves. If her pops were here, sitting in his boat, he'd check the latches, laugh at the three inches of water sloshing around their feet while he cooked up ideas for the next model. Donut clamped her eyes shut, felt the waves swing the bow around.

"Hey, you okay?"

She opened her eyes. They were facing the shore and Tiny was twisted around looking at her.

"It's your pops, isn't it? Want to head back?"

"No, I'm okay."

They sat quietly for a minute, rocking a little in the waves. Donut dipped her hand in the water. "Shoot, might as well be frozen solid. It's that cold."

"Should we try it out?" said Tiny softly.

Donut picked up her paddle and slapped the surface of the pond. "You bet. Now that we're launched I'm gonna name her: the *Nehi*. Let's see how she handles."

They dipped their paddles on opposite sides and eased around and forward, doing a little zigzagging until they balanced out their strokes.

"Why the *Nehi*?" asked Tiny.

"After Pops, her inventor. You know—soda pop. And he always drank peach Nehi and she's about knee-high sitting up on land. It all fits."

"Peach. That's right."

Donut nodded, taking a quick breath at the thought of it.

They rested the paddles across their laps and drifted out over the deepest part of Dog Pond. Donut peered over the side, past the blue-green into the deep where the sunlight couldn't reach, a place full of secrets, where big fish lurked in the cold mud. A dark stillness rose up to the surface, the same forever stillness of the mouse she'd wrapped in red flannel and stowed in her mother's hope chest just a few hours ago.

Tiny whistled softly. "Deep water's so darn quiet."

"Yeah."

Donut pulled back from the water and clutched the paddle in her lap. She checked the latches holding the cedar plank across the fold in the boat and gazed up at Tiny's back. Too bad he was so big. If he was a puny kid like Artie Bellevance, the *Nehi* would float higher in the water. But Artie talked too much and never said anything interesting. If she was gonna sit in the *Nehi* over that deep, dark spot, she'd take Tiny any day.

The paddles dripped. A crow flew overhead, cawing his disapproval. Donut's feet had gone all pink-and-white splotchy from soaking in the icy water in the bottom of the boat.

On the far side of Dog Pond she could just make out Chanticleer, Marcel's cabin, tucked among the cedars. If she did run away it would be the perfect hideout. She'd been there once when she was only six or seven. André, her pops,

Sam, and Marcel had all sat around the table playing poker, telling tall tales about the big fish that got away, the shot that went wide when the six-point buck leaped through the cedars. They'd hiked home in the moonlight, her pops holding her hand, both of them listening to the night noises.

Donut tucked her head down low and curled her toes up in the icy water.

"Let's head back," she said. "Feet are cold."

"Mine, too," said Tiny.

They paddled toward shore, moving quickly through the water, rocks and reeds and mud now visible below. With a final stroke the boat ground up on land. They both had a good feel for the *Nehi* now—where her center was, her touchy spots. Tiny got out without much trouble and Donut followed. They dumped the water out, folded the boat up, pulled on their socks and boots, and carried the boat back to the patch of raspberry canes.

"Nice little boat," said Tiny. "You could fish for perch in her, little stuff, but you couldn't be out in rough weather. Good thinking boat."

"It is," said Donut. "He wasn't done with it, you know. Called this his model A. Fold it up, strap it to the running board of your automobile, and when you saw a good fishing hole you were ready to go."

"Turned out better than I thought," said Tiny, giving her a friendly punch.

On the path back to the road they walked single file, Donut in the lead. She smiled. They'd done it—paddled right to the middle, proved her pops' invention wasn't some pipe dream, a drowning bucket like Mr. Daniels had claimed.

"Hey," she said, "how the heck is Sam going to get that moose out of the parlor when he's finished?"

"I asked him. All he'd say was 'One step at a time, my boy.'"

"Kinda working himself into a corner."

"Yeah," said Tiny. "And he's gotta get it finished and all crated up and delivered to that millionaire's mansion in Newport, Rhode Island, in a couple of weeks."

"That big old moose is gonna scare those flapper-ladies silly."

"That's something I'd pay a nickel to see."

"Me, too," said Donut. "He's bound to start swinging his big rump when the jazz band gets to playing, catching his antlers in the chandelier."

Tiny laughed. "Not much of a rump so far."

"Skinny, headless thing," said Donut. "He should call him Ichabod Crane. The one who got spooked by the headless horseman in that story."

"Ichabod. That's just about the perfect name."

They were both quiet as they continued down the path, jumping over tree roots and puddles. Back on the road, Tiny picked up a few throwing stones and they walked on side by side.

Tiny side-armed a rock at a mossy boulder in the brush. "You got to figure out a way to keep your auntie here."

"First thing is to find her a job so there'd be something to live on," said Donut.

"Not many of those in the village."

"Mrs. Brochu at the Metal Works is older than mud."

"Can your auntie do that kind of work?"

"She manages that school in Boston with Aunt Jo. I bet she'd have Mr. Daniels' place running smooth as soap."

"It's worth a shot."

"I could bring up Mrs. Brochu and her arthritis and the job in an offhand kind of way."

"That's a plan," said Tiny.

Donut kicked at a rock. Aunt Agnes was the last person in the Northern Hemisphere she wanted living in her house. But there was no question about it—having a disagreeable auntie around sure beat moving to Boston and losing everything.

6

Donut knew she had to make up with her auntie before she casually mentioned the perfect job for her at Mr. Daniels' Metal Works. It wasn't easy. With an ill-tempered horse it was best to let them know you were coming and hold out a sugar cube or carrot to get things started. But when Donut got home from Dog Pond there weren't enough carrots in the whole county to settle Aunt Agnes down. So, for what was left of a perfectly good Saturday she delivered up apologies and did extra chores to smooth her auntie's ruffled feathers concerning the bent-hairpin remark and the kicked chair.

Sunday morning Donut dried the last of the breakfast dishes and sat down at the kitchen table across from Aunt Agnes, who was reading another one of Aunt Jo's letters.

They sure had a lot to say to each other. What with her auntie reading up on the latest news from Boston, the timing still wasn't right to bring up Mrs. Brochu and the Metal Works.

"Auntie," said Donut, "I'm going to go visit Sam, see how he's coming along with his moose."

"A moose in the parlor." Aunt Agnes shook her head. "Remarkable."

"He's an artist, really," said Donut. "Worked at the Museum of Natural History in New York City."

"Well, I suppose there is an element of artistry in the final product, but my word, it's gruesome."

"I'm going now. The woodbin's full and I emptied the ashes in the fireplace."

"Don't be in such a rush," said Aunt Agnes. "Let's visit awhile."

"Sure." Donut forced a smile. She figured she'd better pitch a question or two across the table to keep her auntie happy. "What's Aunt Jo got to say in her letter?"

Aunt Agnes smiled back. "It might interest you—a thorny issue at the academy."

"What's so thorny?"

"The older girls are so distracted by all this flapper nonsense—bobbing their hair, sneaking cigarettes in the park."

"Sounds like Doris Barclay."

"Who's Doris?"

"Gus and Hank's sister. She's fourteen. Reads *True Confessions* and bobbed her own hair. Came out awful crooked. The only flapper we've got in the village."

Aunt Agnes sighed. "All my life I've fought for women's rights and these girls . . . Well, we didn't march in the bitter cold and go on hunger strikes in jail cells so they could hem their skirts a few inches higher."

"You were in jail?" Donut stared at her aunt.

"Just the once. We were arrested in Washington, D.C., during a peaceful protest back in 1917. The Silent Sentinels, we were called."

"Why were you protesting?"

"We were trying to convince President Wilson to support the women's suffrage amendment."

"Wowie." Donut stared some more. Aunt Agnes had been in jail, fought for the vote for women. It was hard to square what she was hearing with the auntie she knew in flowered dresses, knitting socks.

"So what are you going to do about the girls sneaking cigarettes?"

"What do you think we should do?"

"Miss Beebe would give them a good whack with her ruler."

Aunt Agnes sat up straight and shook her head. "Absolutely not. We don't believe in corporal punishment."

"Gee," said Donut, "then I don't know."

After some small talk about the weather Donut untangled herself from the visit with her auntie. Carrying her taxidermy tools and supplies in a leather satchel, she headed down to Sam's.

In her stocking feet she watched from his parlor door as he climbed up and down a stepladder. He'd packed clean straw on the rump and midsection of the moose and was wrapping carpet thread around and around the belly to secure it.

"Excellent timing," he said. "Just stand up here and I'll hand you the spool. Too much climbing for an old man."

"Sam, I've got a name for your moose—Ichabod," said Donut. "Skinny and headless, both."

"Ichabod, like in the Headless Horseman, Washington Irving's story." Sam nodded. "I like it."

They worked quietly, handing off the spool of thread, laying down a neat spiral around Ichabod's belly. Up on the ladder, she'd lean over the moose's broad back and drop the spool into Sam's hand, he'd line up the thread, draw it tight in a half hitch, and hand it back on her side of the moose.

"He's gonna be beautiful," said Donut.

"Nice to be working on a large subject for a change," said Sam. "And my fee for Ichabod here will pay the bills for a good while. I'll have more time for my bird-watching."

Donut handed him the spool and he tied it off. She climbed down off the ladder.

"Sam, did you know Aunt Agnes was a suffragette? She was in prison."

"Yes, during the Wilson presidency, I think. Your pops said Agnes and Jo were a formidable pair."

"But Aunt Agnes in jail? Hard to imagine."

"Most people have stories that would surprise you." Sam sat down on the bench next to Ichabod. "Your pops minded his p's and q's around the Boston sisters, as he called them."

Donut turned away from Sam. So what if Aunt Agnes was some kind of hero. It didn't change anything.

"I'm going to work on my blackbird."

"Good, good."

Donut sat at the small bench Sam had set up for her in the corner of the parlor under a large window. She was working on a red-winged blackbird that Bangor the cat had delivered up to Tiny. Sitting in her chair, staring out the window at the green hills encircling the village, calmed her down some.

This had been her special workspace since she was six and she'd brought Sam her first dead mouse and asked him to show her how to fix it. She'd always come here to Sam's after school, until her pops came home from the Metal Works.

Watching Sam work was like going to a magic show. When she was six he'd carried the body of a great horned owl into the parlor. It was enormous—feathers scruffed up, head tipped back over Sam's arm, one wing hanging loose, almost sweeping the floor.

"What happened to him?" she'd asked.

"Marcel found him, dead in the snow. Pretty well starved. Wing's broken, poor fellow."

"Arthur, call him Arthur," she'd said.

And over the next few weeks she'd watched as Sam worked his magic. Now Arthur the great-horned owl sat on the shelf in the mudroom. When she gazed up at him, Donut still wondered what had happened. But perched high on the shelf in a cloud of silence, Arthur held his story close— the story of how he broke his wing, went hungry, and died in the snow.

"Remember, make the body smaller than the original," said Sam, busy packing straw around Ichabod's thick neck.

The skinned blackbird lay on its back on the bench. Donut stroked the velvety feathers. All hollowed out, he needed fixing. She balled up a handful of dry grass and began winding thread around it, as Sam had shown her. In the background she could hear him whispering to Ichabod. He always talked to his animals. She smiled.

This is where she should live. Right here in this house with Sam. He could whisper to her about the history of her pops and she'd whisper back. To earn a living they'd work on more Ichabods together, and she could keep an eye on her house up the road—sweep up the dust, keep the cobwebs down. When she was old enough she could move right back in.

Donut tied off the thread. It was never going to happen, since Sam didn't know how to live with another person. Beryl, Mrs. Lamphere's daughter, walked up the hill from the village a few times a week to help him with the housekeeping. But she always got an earful if she moved a book or a hat or one of his pipes. Half the time he'd tell her to go on home because he didn't want the noise of brooms and pots and pans disturbing his work. "There's no sorting me out," he'd say.

Over the years Donut and Sam had come to an understanding. If she stuck to her workbench and didn't meddle with any of his jars and collecting nets, he didn't mind her much. But often Sam would forget she was sitting right there on her stool in the parlor. "Oh. Hello," he'd say, looking up with a start. His all-alone habits were worn into this house like the hollows worn into the stone steps at the town hall.

She let out a long, quiet sigh to push away the sadness of it and set the straw body down on the bench next to the blackbird's skin. Red-winged blackbirds were noisy things, swooping in, ten or twenty of them together, perching in the reeds, chattering back and forth. "It's not right that you'll be all alone on your perch when I'm done," she whispered. "You're not like Sam. You're gonna get lonely."

"What's that?" called Sam.

"Nothing," said Donut. She stood up and walked over to Ichabod. "I'm working on a plan to stay."

"A plan?" Sam wrinkled up his forehead and gave her a look.

"I'm not gonna poison her or anything. Maybe I can get her to settle here."

"Well, glad to hear there's no poison involved." Sam chuckled.

Donut went back to her workbench and wrapped up the blackbird and its new body. "See you later."

In the mudroom she stopped and gazed up at the great horned owl. "I guess I know how you felt, Arthur," she whispered, "with your broken wing and all. Wish me luck."

In the house Donut found Aunt Agnes in the parlor, knitting. The click-clack of the needles was particularly loud. It was now or never.

"Auntie."

"Yes?" Aunt Agnes kept knitting. Click-clack, click-clack.

"I was thinking . . ."

"Yes?"

"Mrs. Brochu, at the Metal Works, runs the office, takes care of orders and letters and keeping the ledger straight. Her arthritis has really slowed her down, and I bet she'd be thankful to move in with her daughter in Greensboro and have a rest." Donut swallowed hard. "I'm sure Mr. Daniels would hire you on the spot."

Aunt Agnes set her knitting down on the side table and looked up at Donut. "I have a job, thank you very much, and I certainly have no desire to work at a furnace factory."

"What's wrong with the Metal Works? Pops worked there."

"I'm not saying there's anything wrong with it."

"Auntie, you just don't understand. I can't leave. Tiny, Sam, the whole village." Donut chewed at her bottom lip to hold back the tears.

Aunt Agnes shook her head. "I know it's difficult, but you'll adjust."

Donut stared at the ball of gray yarn on the side table. She could wrap it round and round Aunt Agnes like the thread she'd wound around the handful of grass on her workbench at Sam's. She'd find a kind, understanding auntie, stuff this one inside, and sew it up tight. The new Aunt Agnes would surprise everyone in the village by taking over Mrs. Brochu's job at the Metal Works. They'd plant peas in the garden in May, beets and carrots would follow. Tiny would start coming for a second breakfast again before school.

"I've got lessons to finish," she said, and left the parlor.

Donut sat at her desk with the *Rand McNally World Atlas*, second edition, opened up to the map of Minnesota. She pressed her fingertip down on the town of Bemidji, where the Mississippi got its start. The state had so many lakes it looked like a moth-eaten sweater, with all the dots and blobs of blue ink. Minnesotans probably got taught to swim at a young age or they'd all be drowned in no time. She'd be better off in Bemidji. Her pops had taught her to swim. If she had to leave Cobden, she'd adjust to life in Minnesota much better than to a life stuck with her two aunties in Boston.

Donut slammed the *Rand McNally World Atlas*, second edition, shut. She couldn't sit here in her house one more minute with her auntie filling up the parlor. She ran down the stairs and through the kitchen.

"Going up to see Tiny," she said as she stomped into the mudroom.

"Be back before dark," said Aunt Agnes, perched on the wingback chair.

Carrying her fishing rod, Donut headed up the hill to Tiny's. She knocked on the door of the Patoines' farmhouse and pulled it open. The warm air brushed her cheeks.

"Hello?"

"Who's that at the door?" said Mrs. Patoine from the kitchen.

The nine-year-old twins came bouncing into the mudroom, identical in every way.

"It's your girlfriend, Tiny," they said in unison, and busted up giggling.

"Quiet, you two. Get back to your lessons," said Mrs. Patoine.

"Your boyfriend's—" said Josie.

"In the kitchen," finished Stella. And they started giggling again.

Tiny came to the door and pushed the girls away. "You don't keep quiet I'll knock you for a row of carrots, the both of you."

He gave them a look like he just might do it and they trooped back to the kitchen, whispering and jabbing each other with elbows and shoulders.

"Done with the milking?" asked Donut. "Thought we could go for a paddle in the *Nehi*."

"Can't." Tiny shoved his hands in his pockets and stared down at the floor.

"What's wrong?"

"Winnie's gone lame. Must've stepped in a woodchuck hole. Leg's all swollen. Took forever for Dad and me to get her up to the barn."

"Is she gonna be okay?"

"Doctored her up best we could. Hoping a rest will set her to rights."

"Poor Winnie."

"Come on, I'm gonna check on her now." Tiny turned. "*Maman*, we'll be in the barn."

The twins busted up giggling again, and Tiny's seven-year-old sister, Claire, giggled at their giggling.

"Shush," said Mrs. Patoine. "That's fine, Jules, and it's good to see you, Donut, dear."

Tiny pulled on his coat and they slipped out the door.

Donut gave him a squeeze on the arm.

Inside the barn, Bangor, the cat, gave her a suspicious look from his perch on a grain bin. Donut breathed in the complicated smell of the place—lime, manure, straw, wooden planks, cow—an old smell that reminded a person what their nose was good for.

They made their way down the center aisle of the barn, the stanchions empty since the herd was out in the pasture. A lantern hung over one of the horse stalls in the corner.

"Hey, girl," said Donut, as Tiny had taught her. Cows didn't like surprises. Winnie was bedded down in fresh straw. Tiny sat, lifted Winnie's great big head into his lap, and stroked her neck. She was a beautiful animal—light brown with patches of white like continents stretched down her right side and along her rump. Her left hind leg was wrapped in a poultice.

Donut settled herself in the straw next to Tiny, reached out, and scratched Winnie behind the ear. A steady stream of cow slobber was soaking into Tiny's pant leg.

"She's a beauty," said Donut.

He nodded. Tiny looked small, sitting with Winnie, her big body filling the space. Maybe he felt just the right size with these animals. Since they were little kids, he'd been taller than all of them, a big lunk, everyone making cracks, his passage down the street gathering up stares. "The kid's only seven!" "He's only ten. Gonna be a giant." "What're they feeding you, boy?"

Here in the barn, Tiny was just the right size.

"Poor Winnie," said Donut.

"She's just a cow," he said real soft.

"No, she's not. She's your Winnie." Donut socked Tiny on the arm. "And she's gonna be fine."

"Yeah."

They sat in the straw awhile, the lantern sputtered, and Donut shooshed away the flies settling on Winnie's flank.

"I'm thinking of asking Sam to talk to Aunt Agnes," said Donut. "She's really stuck on her job in Boston. Got her nose out of joint when I brought up the Metal Works."

"If anyone can turn her around, Sam's the one. She won't scare him a bit."

"I could ask him to supper. She'd like that."

"Yeah," said Tiny. "Might work."

Winnie twitched her right ear and he gave her a scratch.

Donut stood and brushed the straw off her coat. "I sure hope she's on her feet soon."

"Hey, I'll walk you home."

They were quiet on the way down the hill. At her drive they stopped.

"Don't worry, Winnie'll be fine."

Tiny sagged a little. "See you tomorrow."

Donut watched him hike back up the hill. He didn't pitch a single rock, and his shoulders were all slumped. He'd be checking on Winnie all afternoon, and knowing Tiny, he might just spend the night in the barn to keep an eye on her. At the crest of the hill, his outline was sharp and perfect against the sky for just a second, and then he disappeared down the backside. Donut wrapped her arms around herself. Slapp Hill was just getting sadder and sadder.

Monday morning Donut headed down the hill to school. Tiny was waiting for her on the bridge.

"How's Winnie?"

"About the same," he said. "But she ate some mash this morning."

"Well, that's good."

They walked side by side, Tiny throwing rocks, Donut kicking them into the scrub.

"Did you ask her?" he said. "About the supper?"

"Not yet. After school."

"Listen, Donut." Tiny stopped and looked at her straight on. "This whole thing with your aunties just isn't right. Not after you losing your pops and all." He punched her gently on the arm. "Whatever it takes. We'll keep you here where you belong."

Donut looked away, studied the ruts in the dirt road. "Thanks, Tiny," she whispered.

When they got to the schoolyard, Pudge and the Barclay boys were squatting over a cedar plank under the sugar maple at the far edge of the yard. Donut had her poker stake of twenty pennies tied in one of her pops' red handkerchiefs stuffed deep in her pocket.

"Hey, you're late," said Pudge.

"Deal the cards, boys." Donut balanced her book bag on top of her lunch pail. "Let's play."

Pudge shuffled, his skinny fingers tense, tongue sticking out in concentration. Fumbling the cards, he almost dumped the deck in the dirt at his feet.

"All clear," whispered Stuckie, the lookout, perched on a low branch in the maple.

Donut had tagged along with her pops to Sam's weekly poker games on Friday nights for as long as she could remember. Marcel and André were regulars. She'd sat up on a stack of books piled on a chair in Sam's kitchen and watched as the men laughed and hollered and bluffed their way through every game. At the age of nine she'd been dealt her first hand. When she couldn't keep her eyes open any longer she'd wander into Sam's parlor and curl up in his soft armchair and fall asleep to the strum of cards being shuffled, laughter, and the clink of coins.

After Aunt Agnes arrived Donut had made up a story about suppers at Sam's on Friday nights. No one had ever said a word about her pops' empty chair. They'd just acted like it was a normal Friday night and dealt her in. But secrets never stayed secret in Cobden. Aunt Agnes had heard from Mrs. Stratton what Donut was up to over at Sam's on Friday nights, and that was the end of that.

So she'd started her own poker game. She'd taught the boys at school how to gamble. Up until then, all they'd known was rummy, old maid, horse and pepper, or go fish. The morning poker game had caught on.

Pudge finished dealing the cards and they all squatted around the cedar plank.

"Ante up, Gus," said Donut.

"Don't let her bluff you out of the pot this time," said Wally Ducharme, standing off to the side with his little brother, Pete.

"Yeah," said Pete. They'd both been banned from the game because Pete wouldn't quit slipping his aces to Wally under the cedar plank.

"Shut up, you two," said Pudge.

"Who you telling to shut up?" said Wally.

"Yeah, who?" said Pete.

"We're trying to play cards here," said Pudge.

Wally gave him a good shove with his foot and tipped him over, his face landing in the dirt.

"Hey!" yelled Pudge.

Tiny set his cards down on the plank and stood up. That's all he ever had to do to end any foolishness in the schoolyard. Wally and Pete backed away.

Stuckie's legs started swinging up over their heads. "Stash the cards," he said in a loud whisper. "Beebe's coming."

The spectators scattered. Pudge swept up the cards and shoved them in his lunch pail.

"What are you children doing over here behind this tree again?" Miss Beebe towered over them in her black coat. Donut stared straight ahead at Miss Beebe's skinny legs and studied the stitching that closed up the holes in her black wool stockings. The track down her shin resembled the Nile running backward, with the great delta fanning out around her ankle, where it looked like she'd stitched up a dog bite.

"Just jawing about the weather, ma'am," said Tiny. He stood eye to eye with Miss Beebe, who was a tall woman.

"Jules, I find it hard to believe that talk of the weather would draw such a crowd. I'll be ringing the bell shortly. Get out from behind that tree where I can keep an eye on you scallywags." Miss Beebe turned and headed back to the schoolhouse.

The day took forever to tick by. At noon Tiny complained

of a stomachache and took off for home. Doris and Donut sat at their desks eating lunch.

"What's got into him?" said Doris, pulling a sandwich wrapped in waxed paper out of her pail. "Didn't look too sick to me."

"Got a cow needs tending," said Donut.

They kept on eating, the chatter and laughing of classmates all around them. Donut was quiet, all caught up with the supper and imagining Sam and Aunt Agnes locking horns over their goddaughter.

"You got a sick cow, too?" said Doris, poking Donut with an elbow. "That face could open a tight lid. What's eating you?"

"Nothing."

"Yeah? If it's nothing, it's a whole lot of nothing."

"It's my auntie, that's all. Takes some getting used to."

"I bet. Doesn't mix much with folks. Looked like a squirrel in a trap when I saw Mrs. Lamphere corner her at the post office for a chat."

Donut ate her apple while Doris babbled on. "I read up on Gilda Gray in the latest issue of *True Confessions*. She's the shimmy queen, you know. Lives in Hollywood, California. Can you imagine that?" Doris closed her eyes and sighed. "Oh, wouldn't it just be the cat's whiskers to be a flapper in Hollywood with a long string of pearls?"

Donut shook her head. All Doris wanted was to run off

to New York City or Hollywood or Chicago, while Donut would do anything to stay right here in her little village. Maybe Aunt Agnes would make a trade and haul Doris off to Boston instead of her. Donut smiled at the thought of her auntie trying to civilize Doris.

Considering how the afternoon dragged on through dictation and spelling and poetry, the sun should have set and the moon risen over the hills. Donut sighed louder than she meant to, and Doris giggled. Miss Beebe was never gonna finish up with Henry Wadsworth Longfellow.

After school Donut hiked up Slapp Hill Road alone. She hung her coat on its peg and pulled off her boots. As always, Aunt Agnes was sitting in the parlor in the wing-back chair.

"Auntie," said Donut, trying for a friendly voice. "Can I ask Sam to supper?"

"Supper?" Aunt Agnes looked up from her book.

"I just thought you two should get to know each other better, being my godmother and godfather."

Aunt Agnes's face softened. "Well, wouldn't that be nice."

"He could probably come anytime." Donut swallowed. She was sounding way too eager.

"Is that so?" Aunt Agnes peered at Donut over her

spectacles. "Let's say tomorrow, Tuesday. I'll pick up one of that André fellow's chickens."

"Gosh, that'll be great." Donut leaned against the doorframe, tried to act natural. It was all new, this lying and sneaking around. How did criminals do it—rob banks, hide all that money under their mattresses? Sleeping on top of all that loot would be like snoozing on a porcupine, what with the guilt and the worry poking up through the sheets. Donut figured she just wasn't cut out for a life of crime.

"Ask him to come at six." Aunt Agnes smiled and stood up. "Now, Aunt Jo and I have a surprise for you. Sit down for a minute."

Donut sat on the straight-backed chair by the fire. Her aunties' last big surprise had been news of a kidnapping coming up in two weeks. What had they cooked up now? A trunk full of petticoats, ribbons, and white gloves?

Aunt Agnes trundled over to the writing desk, picked up a package, and handed it to her with a big grin. Donut tried for a smile and did a pretty good job of it.

The package was wrapped in brown paper with stamps and string and her name on it. The return address was Miss Jo Dabney at the Winslow Academy for Girls in Boston. The heft of it gave it away right off. A book. A large one. Probably one of Aunt Agnes's dry-as-a-chip histories or biographies. Donut untied the string and pulled off the brown paper.

In her lap was the *Rand McNally World Atlas*, third edition.

She looked up. Aunt Agnes stood there, her grin even bigger.

"I asked Sam what you might like. He said you'd been saving for a long while for just this book. Jo and I wanted to get you something special."

"Thank you." It came out stiff as a starched collar.

Her auntie's grin sagged. "What's wrong?"

Donut stared down at the *Rand McNally World Atlas*, third edition. She'd been saving for more than a year now, only two dollars short of her goal. She'd only told Sam, Tiny, and her pops. Aunt Agnes had no business nosing around, uncovering her secrets and private hopes and stealing them.

Donut was quiet. She couldn't pretend, couldn't "ooh" and "ah" over the gift just to keep her auntie in a good mood for the supper with Sam.

Aunt Agnes put her hands on her hips and snorted like a winded horse. "Well, that's not the reaction I was expecting."

Donut was quiet.

Aunt Agnes left the room in a huff. But right before she turned away Donut caught the hurt in her aunt's eyes, just a flash of it beneath the anger.

Donut sat and stared at the beautiful book, bound in maroon leather, with the title set in a frame of gold curlicues.

Gritting her teeth, she got up and hurried past Aunt Agnes in the kitchen. In her room, she plunked down on her bed, set the *Rand McNally World Atlas*, third edition, on her lap, and ran her hand across the cover.

She had to open it, just the once. Breathe in the wondrous smell of new ink and crisp, fresh paper. Flipping through the pages, she found the map of Egypt. The brilliant blue of the Mediterranean popped right off the page. She traced the Nile River with her finger as it snaked across the desert and split into the Rosetta and Damietta mouths, forming the great Nile Delta. The delta didn't hold just a collection of pearls—it was the Hope diamond—packed tight with towns and villages.

Donut slammed the *Rand McNally World Atlas*, third edition, shut. It was bait. She might as well be a hungry lake trout circling a fat, juicy worm stuck on a fishhook. Her auntie had crept around, found out her deepest desire, and stolen it. And Sam, that snake in the grass, had told her.

She should march out the door, hike up to Dog Pond, paddle the *Nehi* out to the deep spot, and drop it overboard. Give the *Rand McNally World Atlas*, third edition, the deep six for the edification of all the fish lurking at the muddy bottom.

Donut scowled at the thought of it. She couldn't really drown any book, no matter its traitorous origins. But she was never, ever gonna crack this one open again. She picked up the heavy book, opened her closet door, and shoved it deep in the back, on the floor with the boots and dust and spiders.

Donut slammed the closet door shut and charged down the stairs and through the kitchen.

"Going out," she said to her aunt.

"Out? Where?"

Donut was out the door before Aunt Agnes had time to slow her down. With her boots untied, her running was mostly shuffling. But she couldn't stop and tie them. She was in too much of a hurry to give Sam a piece of her mind.

Her right foot pulled halfway out of her boot and she swung her arms so as not to tip over, which sucked some of the steam out of her. If she stepped too high she might just float and flap away from the Earth, her boots stuck fast in the mud. They'd find them empty and there'd be quite a mystery in Cobden for years to come.

CALEDONIA GAZETTE

Girl Gone Missing

APRIL 19, 1927

THE MYSTERIOUS DISAPPEARANCE OF AN ELEVEN-YEAR-OLD GIRL, DOROTHY SEDGEWICK, AKA DONUT, ON SLAPP HILL ROAD WAS REPORTED MONDAY AFTER-NOON. IT APPEARS THAT SHE STOPPED

DEAD IN HER TRACKS, TOOK THE TIME
TO UNLACE HER BOOTS AND VANISHED
IN HER STOCKING FEET. HER SIZE-SIX
LEATHER BOOTS ARE ALL THAT REMAIN.
ANYONE WITH ANY INFORMATION SHOULD
CONTACT SERGEANT ERNIE MAYO AT THE
COBDEN TOWN OFFICES.

It might even make the *Burlington Free Press.* She guessed it was better than dying in her sleep, all old and gray, with no teeth in her head. When old people died in their sleep, was it right in the middle of a dream?

Donut slogged down the hill.

Standing in his mudroom, she gave a good strong yell. "Sam?"

She shuffled into the parlor in her muddy boots. Ichabod stood there, bigger than before, white as a marble statue—a ghost moose. Sam had finished the first coat of papier-mâché and the skull was attached now, turned to the right, staring through empty eye sockets out the window over her workbench. His huge antlers curved upward, almost touching the ceiling. The moose had weight now, the right hind leg and the left front leg ahead of their partners, standing on four solid hoofs.

Donut moved closer, stretched out her hand, and laid it on Ichabod's shoulder. It was damp to the touch. She couldn't imagine trying to sleep in the house once he was a proper moose, with his skin on and glass eyes in. She'd just lie in bed thinking of the stomping and banging Ichabod would make if he got loose from the board, punching holes in the pine floor, busting windows with his antlers, smacking dents in the plaster walls with that enormous rump.

Donut laced her boots up tight and headed out the door. Sam's old house sat at the edge of a thirty-acre hayfield bordered by a twenty-acre woodlot. In good weather he'd cart his canvas fold-up chair out into the milkweed and canary grass and sit with his binoculars spying on bobolinks and finches, writing up bird habits in his notebook with a sharp pencil.

She understood how much he loved his birds, and he should have understood what the *Rand McNally World Atlas*, third edition, meant to her and kept his mouth shut.

The ground was muddy and the grass still short, what with the cold nights. Sam was nowhere in sight. Donut followed the trail into the woods. Tiny and the Barclay boys had built him a tree stand—a platform fifteen feet off the ground, with slats for climbing nailed into the trunk of the old beech tree. She caught sight of his boots hanging off the edge.

"Sam."

"Donut? Climb up, but quiet, please."

She climbed up the slats and pulled herself onto the

platform. Sam had his notebook in his lap and a pencil stuck over his ear. She sat down next to him, her legs hanging.

"Sam," she said.

"Shhhh," he said, staring off into the thick woods surrounding the clearing.

"No. I'm not gonna 'shhh.' You told Aunt Agnes about the *Rand McNally World Atlas*, third edition."

Donut sniffled. Her nose was running. She held on tight to the rough edge of the platform. Being angry at Sam, who she'd known her whole life, meant she was all alone, fifteen feet up, sitting right next to him.

He set his notebook and pencil down on the cedar planking. "She only wanted to get you a gift, something special. I knew your heart was set on getting the third edition."

"But it's my heart, Sam, my secret. And you told her. I was saving up. My poker winnings. It was private, none of their business, and she and Aunt Jo went and bought it. They ruined it. I can't ever look inside now because they stole it from me."

Sam gazed at her, his eyebrows twitching. Donut mopped at her runny nose with her coat sleeve. They both stared down into the clearing.

"I'm sorry," said Sam. "It was a mistake."

"It's way bigger than a mistake."

"Hmmm."

Donut turned and glared at him. "Why do adults make that sound? 'Hmmm.' It's like a long lecture about how to be a proper child all squashed into one little squeak."

Sam smiled. "It is, isn't it? I'll try to avoid squeaking at you. Not very respectful."

"My geography's like your birds, Sam," said Donut.

He patted her on the knee. "And it's grand, isn't it?"

Donut shoved her hands into her pockets.

Sam gently got hold of her chin and swung her face around to look at him. "I will try my best not to betray your trust again. Promise."

"Okay," she said, just to get him to stop looking at her because the tears were close again.

He picked up his notebook. A pair of black-capped chickadees hopped from branch to branch a few feet away, farther off a downy woodpecker started in hammering at a dead limb of a maple tree.

They watched a crow land on the lower branch of a poplar; another crow joined it, and then another. Sam perked up, tipped his head.

In most cases the job of godfather didn't mean much except a nickel for penny candy and a pat on the head. But Sam had been a special case. She'd grown up in his parlor with his birds, sat in his kitchen with her pops eating stewed apples, watched them play loud games of cribbage.

When she'd turned up an orphan, Sam's job of being her godfather had gotten real serious. He'd come to get her at school, sat her down on the bench in the schoolyard, told her Pops had died. It hadn't made any sense. Her pops, dead. The tire had blown out. The old green Franklin swerved, hit a tree. Her pops had flown up and out into the air, hit his head. And he was gone.

She hadn't cried. Even when Sam had put his arm around her. Because it just didn't make any sense. Sam had walked her home. Held her hand all the way up Slapp Hill Road. For the whole four days before the funeral he stayed with her. Each day she believed her pops was going to walk in the front door, hang up his coat, and give her a hug. He'd be so happy to be back, he'd pick her up in the air and swing her around.

Beryl and Mrs. Lamphere and Mrs. Patoine and all of them brought food and sat in the parlor holding handkerchiefs. Sam kept them away while she worked on the pearls of the Nile, hour after hour, learning the towns and cities, waiting for it all to be a mistake and her pops to come home.

But he didn't. Aunt Agnes arrived the day of the funeral. Sam went back to his parlor and his birds. That was when she knew her pops wasn't coming back.

Donut swung her legs and dug her thumbnail into the cedar board under her hand.

The crows erupted off the poplar tree, squawking and circling. Sam scribbled something in his notebook, set it aside, and lit up his pipe. Donut sat kind of stiff and her stomach started to ache.

"Sam, can you come to supper, tomorrow at six? Maybe

you could get Aunt Agnes to see that I have to stay put, that I'd never survive in Boston."

Sam chewed on the end of his pipe. "Of course I'll come to supper. And I'll think long and hard about what might persuade her to change her mind."

"She wouldn't even think about taking a job at the Metal Works. I tried."

He chuckled. "No, I just guess she wouldn't. Not her cup of tea."

"But she'd listen to you, being Pops' best friend, and you knowing me forever and being my godfather and all."

Sam shook his head. "Don't get your hopes up."

"I just can't go," said Donut, her voice all wobbly.

He looked at her hard, reached over, and squeezed her hand. "I miss him, too, Donut. I'll do my best."

Donut managed to mumble some kind of thanks and a goodbye while she scrambled to her feet. She had to leave, and quick. Sitting there with Sam brought on a wave of missing her pops so powerful she could hardly make her legs work to climb down the slats. She stood for a minute on solid ground and pushed the ache back down into a hidden, deep place so she could keep breathing and walking and being in the world.

10

Donut hiked back across Sam's field. Aunt Agnes was probably sitting at the kitchen table sipping at her tea, all hurt and angry that the *Rand McNally World Atlas*, third edition, hadn't gotten her a big thank-you and a kiss on the cheek.

Donut kicked at a clump of burdock. Aunt Agnes had been brave and heroic, even gone to jail for what she believed in. Donut didn't like her auntie one bit, but the longer she sat in the parlor knitting those ugly socks, the more complicated the not liking her got. Why couldn't she have an auntie who was a battle-ax, a witch with a raggedy, old-fashioned broomstick leaning against the wall in the mudroom? With an aunt like that, Donut could heave her over a cliff, put arsenic in her tea, cast her own spell and turn her into a frog or a spider, and do a dance out of pure happiness afterward.

Donut studied her house across the road. All she could do with the auntie she had was stand aside and hope Sam could work a miracle.

In the mudroom she pulled on her slippers and stood in the doorway to the kitchen. Aunt Agnes must have heard her come in, but she didn't turn away from the stove.

"I'd like the parlor dusted," she said, giving Donut a good view of her behind and the neat bow of her blue apron strings tied up tight. "And you have schoolwork to attend to."

Donut's "Yes, Auntie" barely made it into the open air. She had to soften Aunt Agnes up for the big dinner, so she pinched herself on the arm and managed a friendly voice. "And I'm sorry about the atlas. It's beautiful."

Aunt Agnes turned and put her hands on her hips. "Your sorrys are getting tiresome."

The both of them being angry sucked the air right out of the room. Donut rummaged in the hall closet and gathered up a rag and feather duster.

In the parlor, she lifted the little statues and knickknacks, wiped down the shelves with her cloth, dusted the picture frames and lamps. This had been her mother's special room. All of it came from the house in Boston where Rose had grown up with Aunt Agnes and Aunt Jo. Donut and her pops had hardly ever used the parlor. He'd kept the door closed and only went in to tidy up and set traps since the quiet encouraged mice to nest in the cushions.

Now Aunt Agnes was in here every day, perched on the dainty chair at the skinny-legged desk writing all her letters to Aunt Jo, or sitting in the wingback chair with her books and knitting. This room wasn't supposed to have Aunt Agnes in it. It wasn't supposed to have anyone in it. Just her pops' memories of her mother, Rose.

She stood in the center of the room on her mother's carpet filled with tiny woven animals—camels, birds, snakes, and lizards, all in reds and blues and yellows. Her pops said he'd carted her in here special to learn to crawl on this carpet, safe from splinters, her little fingers getting some traction on the soft bumpiness of the wool.

Feather duster in one hand, rag in the other, Donut sat down on the carpet and lay on her back. The ceiling hung there above her, ivory white, with black cracks in the plaster like bare winter branches.

Her mother was drifting away now, disappearing. Donut could lie here and remember her pops and how he'd laughed and snapped his suspenders, but her pops wasn't here to hang on to Rose for the both of them. "She'd pull her socks and shoes off any chance she got," he'd said, smiling at the thought of it. "Sink in the mud with her head back, admiring the sky."

Aunt Agnes was Rose's big sister. Aunt Jo, too. But their

memories had nothing to do with Donut, nothing to do with her pops. She'd lost her mother for good now. The ache of it was fierce, and she dug her fingers into the carpet.

"What are you doing lying there?" said Aunt Agnes, standing at the door.

Donut sat up, rattled by her auntie's voice. When a person was miles upriver in their own thoughts, it was only polite to cough before barging in and giving them a shock.

"Looking for cobwebs," she said, scrambling to her feet.

"Well, looking won't get the job done," said Aunt Agnes.

Donut gazed down at the carpet, where a whole army of woolen beasts was ready to leap up and do her bidding. Like a tiny cavalry, the camels and snakes and lizards would swarm up Aunt Agnes's legs and drive her screaming from the house.

"I'll get it done," she said.

Her auntie's lips went thin and straight at the choke-cherry sour in Donut's voice. "I'm sure you have schoolwork to do, so finish up."

"Yes, Auntie."

Aunt Agnes turned and left. Donut put the rag and feather duster back in the hall closet and, without a word, walked through the kitchen and up the stairs to her room.

She crawled into bed under her quilt. When she got rid of Aunt Agnes, she'd have to get herself a dog. The house wouldn't be peaceful quiet, just empty quiet. A home needed more than one living thing breathing in the air, bumping up the stairs. A yawn wasn't any good if there wasn't someone else to pick up on it and yawn, too.

Donut shut her eyes. What with knowing the *Rand McNally World Atlas*, third edition, was collecting dust on the floor in her closet, worrying about Tiny and his Winnie, and her whole future depending on one chicken supper, she was worn thin.

She fell asleep, a deep middle-of-the-night sleep, curled up, her knees almost touching her chin.

"Dorothy. It's suppertime."

Donut sat up, dragged out of a dream. "What?"

Aunt Agnes stood at her door, a wooden spoon in one hand. "It's suppertime. I've been calling you."

Still fuzzy-headed, she followed her auntie downstairs and set the bread and butter on the table. Aunt Agnes filled up two bowls with soup from the pot on the stove. At the table, Donut was quiet, focused on buttering her bread, trying to wake up properly. Of course, the soup was chock-full of turnips. It was always turnips. Donut stared at them, sunken down at the bottom of her bowl. Woody and tasteless, they sucked the life out of everything they touched.

"You've worn yourself out," said Aunt Agnes, shaking her head. "Running all over the countryside for days. We'll clean up the kitchen and make an early night of it."

"I am kind of tired."

Donut stared down at her almost empty bowl. It wasn't the running. She could run all the way to Montpelier, say hello to the governor, and skip back home and she wouldn't get close to this kind of tired. This heavy-headed tired was from juggling worries, like the carnival act in Barton when the man in the blue tights juggled flaming torches, four of them all at the same time, while everyone in the audience held their breath 'til they might just pass out.

"Dorothy?"

"I'm fine, Auntie," Donut stood up to clear the table. "Really."

But she wasn't fine. Not one bit fine, what with flaming torches whistling over her head.

11

Tuesday was a rotten day at school. Tiny'd shown up late and said that Winnie was still doing poorly. He'd wished Donut luck with the dinner, but his sad face didn't look too lucky.

When Donut got home the smell of roasted chicken filled up every free crack and corner. Aunt Agnes turned away from the stove and wiped her hands on her apron. "How was school?"

"Fine," said Donut.

"I'm sure you have lessons to do."

Upstairs in her room, Donut did her best not to think about the supper despite the smell of roasting chicken. She was worried about Tiny, too, and Winnie. Sitting at her desk, she did the page of arithmetic problems that she'd copied from the blackboard. She didn't need to bother with the geography lesson. She'd learned all the states and capitals two years ago, when her pops had given her the *Rand McNally World Atlas*, second edition.

The oddest state capital was Pierre, South Dakota. Just plain old Pierre—French for Peter. It was like naming the capital of Vermont Charlie or Jack. Who had this Pierre been? Had he known Teddy Roosevelt? She'd read up on Teddy in one of Sam's books. T.R. had run off and become a cowboy in the Dakota Territory, living on a ranch, hunting buffalo, and going to saloons. He could skin a mouse in minutes, stuffed and mounted birds he'd shot, rode bareback, and survived in the wilderness.

Donut pulled the P–Q volume of the *Encyclopedia Britannica* off her shelf and began shuffling through the pages, looking for Pierre, South Dakota.

"Dorothy," called Aunt Agnes. "Time to set the table."

Donut set the P–Q volume aside, brushed her hair, and pulled on a dress and clean socks. She'd show Aunt Agnes that she didn't need any civilizing in the big city. And Sam might just pull off a miracle between bites of chicken and gravy.

Aunt Agnes fussed at the stove while Donut set the table with her mother's good china. She hoped Sam wasn't still at work on Ichabod, up to his elbows in papier-mâché. Being Sam, he might very well show up late with straw in his hair, or forget altogether about the supper invitation.

She set the salt and pepper shakers down on the table with two clunks. They were echoed by knocks on the door, and she raced into the mudroom. There he stood, a work of art—slicked-down hair, a wool suit, bow tie, and city shoes.

"Wowie," said Donut.

"Needed to make the proper impression," he whispered.

In the kitchen Aunt Agnes yanked off her apron, letting loose the flowers on her dress.

"Agnes, this house smells like heaven." He was greasing the wheels real good.

"Can't go wrong with roasted chicken, Sam."

Aunt Agnes and Donut set the chicken and potatoes and peas out on the table and they all sat down.

"Sam, would you like to carve the bird?" said Aunt Agnes.

"I'd be glad to."

Donut figured Sam would be expert at slicing up a chicken, considering his line of work, but she kept it to herself, as Aunt Agnes thought taxidermy a ghoulish profession. He did indeed carve up that bird with absolute confidence.

They were quiet for a while, concentrating on passing the peas, buttering bread, pouring gravy, and trying out the first bites.

"So, Sam," said Aunt Agnes. "How did you meet Dorothy's father?"

Sam glanced up from his plate, looking a bit startled. "Well, Jake came to New York back around 1910 to consult at the Museum of Natural History, where I worked. He was brilliant at designing armatures, the metal and wooden inner workings needed for the larger animals—wildebeests, rhinos, elephants. As a self-taught engineer, he was a big help."

"Wildebeests, my word," said Aunt Agnes, setting down her knife and fork. "And how did you end up being neighbors?"

"I moved up here in 1912. When Mr. Daniels started the Metal Works and was looking for an innovative designer, I contacted Jake. He got the job, and as you know, he and Rose arrived in 1915."

"Dear Rose," said Aunt Agnes in a faraway voice that Donut had never heard before. The room went still for just a moment. All her auntie's sadness and her missing of her sister Rose was packed so tight into those two words it about knocked Donut over. But then Aunt Agnes sat up straight, pushed her shoulders back, and swept it all away. "But that was years ago."

Donut swallowed hard and concentrated on loading up her fork with peas, relieved that her hard-edged auntie had returned.

Sam buttered a slice of bread. "And how did you and your sister get involved with teaching?"

"We're both committed to advancing the education of and prospects for young girls. I've been an administrator at the academy for many years, and Jo taught Latin and Greek. She was named headmistress three years ago. The school is very progressive."

"How interesting," said Sam.

They moved on into a long stretch of small talk, and Donut had to curl her toes and hunch her shoulders to keep quiet and hold out for the only topic she was interested in. After more chewing and passing of the gravy and the peas, Sam finally got down to business.

"So, I hear from Donut that you plan on returning to Boston."

"Yes, and once Dorothy gets used to the idea, we're sure she'll enjoy the academic challenge, along with the cultural enrichments available to her in Boston—museums, concerts, lectures."

"She is a bright girl, full of curiosity. But she has so many attachments here—the village, schoolmates. Have you considered the possibility of settling in Cobden, allowing her to remain, giving her the comfort of a place she knows?"

Aunt Agnes hacked at her chicken leg. The knife dinged against her plate. "Jo and I know very well that this move will be challenging for Dorothy. I appreciate your concern, but we will decide what's best."

Donut stuffed a forkful of potatoes in her mouth to help with keeping quiet. Here she was sitting right at the table between the two of them and she might as well be a dead squirrel two crows were fighting over, for all she was expected to offer on the future of her very own life. Sam continued.

"Yes, yes, I do apologize for bringing it up. Of course it's your decision." He wiped his mouth with his napkin and scratched at the back of his head. Donut could see the signs of fluster starting up—his hair was beginning to lose its civilized appearance and there was a large gravy stain on his shirt shaped like Lake Michigan.

But he kept at it like a dog with a bone. "I considered Jake a close friend. He was well-liked in Cobden, and we've all been keeping an eye out for Donut since he died."

"And I'm sure Dorothy appreciates the support, but life does go on." Aunt Agnes worried her potatoes, mashed at them with her fork. "I assure you that we have her best interests at heart. And of course Jo and I have to earn a living, and we're established in Boston."

Both Aunt Agnes and Sam got busy again with their suppers. This was not going well. "Established." Her aunties were established all right, unmovable, like the bronze statue of General George Washington she'd seen with her pops in the Boston Public Garden.

If she did get dragged to Boston, it would be only fitting if Aunt Agnes should go sleepwalking one night, climb up on a granite block in the park, and turn into bronze, Aunt Jo right next to her, each of them holding up a knitting needle like a sword, green-tinted from the rain, staring out at the passersby, pigeons sitting on their heads and shoulders, cooing and preening their feathers. Bird droppings would trickle down her aunties' backs and bosoms like Mrs. Lamphere's boiled icing on the chocolate cakes she brought to chicken suppers at the Methodist church on High Street. Donut smiled. Free of the both of them, she'd wave goodbye and get on the first train back home.

Sam finished up his meal in silence, set his knife and fork down, and scrubbed at his head with both hands. His eyebrows twitched as he geared up for another assault. "Well, if Donut stayed with me I know Mrs. Lamphere and Beryl, her daughter, would provide a womanly touch to my clumsy bachelor parenting, but we could give it a go. There's plenty of room, and she could go to Boston for school holidays."

Donut pulled in a deep breath. She'd argued herself out of even hoping, tried to keep her distance from wishing that Sam would take her in. And now he'd said it. All on his own. She was welcome to move right in. The dinner had worked a miracle—thank goodness for André's plump chickens and Sam in his city shoes. He'd be so much better than a big dog. And he was all educated and adult and had known her since she was born and he'd known her mother and her pops, so living with him would be like changing trains but still heading in the same direction, still rattling along on the same set of tracks.

"That is a kind offer," said Aunt Agnes, stiffening a little, throwing her shoulders back. "And Dorothy, I hope you appreciate the kindness Sam is showing you tonight, but of course it would never do. We are her guardians, and Dorothy has a bright future. Women are making great strides in all fields now. For goodness' sake, we have the vote. The world is wide open—she could go to university, have a career—and at the academy, she will get the start she needs."

Donut couldn't believe what she was hearing. Aunt Agnes hadn't even stopped to think about Sam's offer. Donut pushed her plate away. Stared at her auntie. There was no point anymore in being polite, complimenting the chicken.

"Mr. Calvin Coolidge, the president of the United States, started out just fine right here in Vermont," Donut said in an ice-cold voice. "And I can vote in the Cobden Town Hall when I'm old enough."

"Dorothy."

Donut got up from her seat and glared at her auntie. Sam had given it his best shot, but there'd been no hope from the start. She slammed both hands down on the table. What was left of the chicken jumped.

"My name is Donut."

"Dorothy," said Aunt Agnes, her face pink, eyes wide. "Behave yourself."

"I am going to live with Sam!"

"Donut," said Sam softly, "sit down."

"I will handle this, if you don't mind." Aunt Agnes turned and glared at Donut. "Sit down this instant."

"No."

Donut wanted to smash her mother's good china, grind the peas and potatoes and chicken skin into the floorboards. She was just a sack of onions with no choices, no nothing. She sagged a little at the nothingness, turned, and climbed the stairs to her room.

"You will stay there until you're ready to apologize," called Aunt Agnes.

Donut sat on her bed, heard Sam say his goodbyes, and listened to Aunt Agnes washing the dishes. She pulled her quilt up around herself, tried to breathe. Sam had offered to take her in, which was bigger than one of the pyramids in Egypt, and Aunt Agnes had dismissed it, turned her camel around and headed back where she'd started, not bothering to even consider one of the Seven Wonders of the World.

Donut took a swing at her pillow. Aunt Agnes was gonna have to ride that camel back to Boston alone. And she, Donut, was going to be sitting in Sam's kitchen with the woodstove roaring, their own darn chicken kicking out real homey smells all through his house. But first, like she'd figured all along, she'd have to take a page out of Teddy Roosevelt's book—run off, live in the wild woods until Aunt Agnes and Aunt Jo decided she wasn't worth the bother.

12

Donut pulled the rope ties loose on her pops' army duffel bag. She packed the *Rand McNally World Atlas*, second edition, the photo of her and her pops in the silver frame, warm clothes, and the Ovaltine can where she kept her poker winnings. She shoved the duffel into the closet and sat down at her desk to write her auntie a letter.

April 19, 1927

Dear Aunt Agnes,

    I have run away. I'm not coming back. I will be safe because I have a plan. I'm sorry that I had to run away since I don't want to worry you or Sam or Tiny or anyone else. But I have no choice.

Say hello to Aunt Jo when you get back to Boston.
I know you were trying to be a proper godmother and all. It
just didn't work out.

Yours truly,
Donut

She changed into her nightclothes, pulled on her
mother's sleeping cap, and climbed into bed. It would have
been easier to run away right then, when she'd built up a
full head of steam. But it was dark and she needed supplies
and a hideout.

She didn't plan on running far, not like Teddy Roosevelt, who'd made it all the way to the Dakotas. He'd been a
lot older, and his family knew where he was even if they
couldn't get there very fast if he needed rescuing. She was
going to be on her own, with no cowboys around or saloons
to visit.

First thing in the morning she'd hike out to Marcel's
place. Chanticleer, his cabin on Dog Pond, was the perfect
hideout. And the *Nehi* was there. If Marcel said no, she
could sleep in Mr. Hollis's falling-down barn on Kate
Brook Road. But it was wide open, with no solid doors or
windows and a poplar tree growing right through a hole in
the roof.

Donut rolled over and pulled the covers up around her
chin.

Tiny might never forgive her for not telling him. But he'd have a terrible time lying to his folks. He'd turn to mush if Aunt Agnes got ahold of him. Sam would be after him, too. It was for his own good she wasn't telling him. Donut kicked at the covers. Tiny wasn't going to like it.

"Tough luck," she whispered.

Donut twisted around under the covers and got her feet tangled up.

Even if she got found out she'd run away all over again, show her aunties that she was just too much trouble. They'd tell Sam he could have her, and good riddance.

She got herself untangled, curled up in a ball, and waited until she heard Aunt Agnes climb the stairs and go into her room, Pops' room, now filled up with old-lady dresses and hats. Donut waited some more, listened as drawers opened and shut, the bed creaked. At long last, the soft rattle of her auntie's snoring drifted through the wall. It was time.

In her stocking feet, Donut hauled the duffel bag down the stairs. In the kitchen she lit the lamp, opened the cupboards, and pulled out four cans of evaporated milk, an almost full can of Ovaltine, crackers, and three cans of sardines. She wrapped up a wedge of cheddar cheese from the pantry box, along with a chunk of salt pork for frying up fish she planned on catching. She packed all of her provisions in the duffel along with a dozen winter apples from the crate in the mudroom, a box of matches, and a handful of candles.

Donut pulled on her boots, and hauled her duffel and fishing rod outside and hid them behind the woodpile.

Back in the house she crept up the stairs and climbed into bed.

~ ~ ~ ~ ~ ~ ~ ~ ~ ~

She didn't remember falling asleep, but when she woke up she was ready to run away. Donut made her bed, folded up her nightclothes and stuffed them in her book bag along with her slippers.

At the kitchen table she poured extra maple syrup on her oatmeal. Aunt Agnes sipped her tea and didn't look up once from her book as Donut ate her breakfast.

She cleared her dishes, pulled on her coat and boots, and swung her book bag over her shoulder. At the door Donut mumbled a quick goodbye to Aunt Agnes and hurried outside. A person said goodbye to someone with an understanding of how long the goodbye was for—a day, a week, a year. The goodbye she gave her auntie was a crummy lie since she wasn't going to school and wouldn't be home to do her chores.

"Too bad," she said.

Donut lugged her gear out to the road. The leaving part should have been more complicated—climbing down a drainpipe or leaping out a window onto a tree branch, not just walking up Slapp Hill like she'd done a thousand times before.

"What do you want?" Donut muttered to herself. "A send-off with real live elephants and a brass band?"

Halfway up the hill she started to feel more like a runaway.

"I did it," she said, and grinned. "Chanticleer will be perfect."

As she passed the Patoine farm she picked up her pace as best she could with the heavy duffel bag banging into her legs. She'd left extra early so she wouldn't run into Tiny heading to the bridge to meet her.

The herd of Guernseys was out in the pasture along the road. A few cows looked up at her as she passed. Donut searched for Winnie, for the distinctive patch of white fur shaped like South America that ran from her chest down her front leg. Winnie wasn't there. Tiny must be in the stall with her, sitting in the straw, telling her she'd be on her feet soon in that voice he had that made you think it was a sure thing. And here she was, running off when her best friend could sure use a good sock on the arm and a smile.

Donut set the duffel down in the dirt, turned, and gazed at the barn. "I just couldn't tell you, Tiny," she whispered.

13

At the turnoff to Dog Pond, Donut stashed her gear and returned to the road.

It was a hike out to Marcel's place. At the top of Bridgeman Hill she turned onto the long dirt track to his house. His roadster had cut deep trenches in the mud. She skipped over puddles and shivered in the shadowy, wet woods, pulling her hat down over her ears.

Marcel's two very large dogs had a reputation for being ferocious, which discouraged trespassers. His chunk of Vermont was wild forest, hundreds of acres of it, just sitting there with no buckets hanging on the sugar maples or cows in the clearings.

He was a trapper in the winter, but ever since alcohol had been made illegal with Prohibition he'd been doing a bit of rum-running in the summer. She was hoping Marcel's law-breaking ways would tilt him toward making a loan of his cabin to a fugitive.

Donut began to whistle every few steps. A strong whistle. A no-nonsense, get-over-here whistle. She kept walking and whistling until she heard Lafayette and Rochambeau hurtling through the woods, busting dead branches, scrabbling through the brush, howling and growling.

"Hey, boys," she called. "Come on, puppies, it's me, Donut."

They tore through the ruts on the track, huge dogs, stiff brown-and-black fur sticking out like bristles on a bottlebrush, wagging their tails at the sight of her.

Donut crouched down and they licked her face, gave it a good scrub, shoved and pushed for a scratch behind the ears, knocking the loneliness and worry right out of her. She fell backward in the mud and laughed as they sat back on their haunches, tongues out, waiting for her to get up.

"You're just too darn big, the two of you," she said, getting back on her feet.

She continued on, escorted by the Generals, as Marcel called them. Donut had read up on the originals in her *Encyclopedia Britannica*. The Count of Rochambeau and the Marquis of Lafayette had sailed over from France to help George Washington win the American Revolution.

Coming around the bend, she saw Marcel's homestead— a small house along with a ramshackle barn. He was sitting on the porch lacing up his boots. The Generals raced up to him and barked to announce her arrival.

"Settle down, the two of you," he said, shoving them aside. "I see you've brought me la *petite* Napoleon."

She plunked down on a bench next to him. Marcel had a way of twisting up his *r*'s and spitting out his *t*'s with his French-Canadian accent that she admired. He'd called her Napoleon ever since she'd won her first hand of poker at Sam's. She'd read up on Napoleon. His dream had been to rule the world no matter what the world wanted. She was glad this particular nickname hadn't caught on.

Lafayette came over and put his head in her lap.

"We've missed you at Sam's Friday nights," said Marcel.

"Aunt Agnes doesn't approve of gambling."

"Some don't, it's the truth."

The Generals wagged their tails, beating out a rhythm on the porch floor.

"She's gonna drag me off to Boston. For good."

"I heard about this from Sam."

"I'm not going."

Donut scrubbed at Lafayette's ears with both hands. She looked over at Marcel, who never seemed to be in need of the back and forth that made up a conversation. She just had to spit it out. Ask him about Chanticleer. But if he said no she was stuck with Mr. Hollis's barn, which had a haunted look to it. She dug her fingers into Lafayette's thick coat.

"Sam offered to take me in. For me to live with him, and she said no."

Marcel eyed her closely. "Your *tante* Agnes, she's your mother's sister, yes? Doesn't beat you. Doesn't starve you."

"I just can't go, Marcel."

"It's a hard one, *ma petite*. The Generals and I are going to miss you. But your *tante*, she's your family now."

"I hardly know her."

Marcel swept his hand down Rochambeau's back, and the dog set his giant head on his knee.

He was going to say no to Chanticleer. He was going to put a stop to her running off before she even got rolling. And if she managed to lug her stuff all the way to Kate Brook Road, the weather could turn—rain, a cold spell. It would be hard to stick it out, what with the night noises and the drip-drip of the rain through Mr. Hollis's barn roof.

She couldn't ask Marcel because when he said no, sneaking off to Chanticleer anyway would be a much worse crime than hiding out there without asking.

"Miss Beebe's rung her school bell by now," said Marcel in a soft voice. "It's early for a visit with the Generals. Why are you here, *ma petite*?"

"Oh, I don't know. Turned right instead of left." Donut swallowed and looked away.

Marcel tilted his head and gazed at her. She needed to change the subject double-quick.

"Sam's moose has got his head on now," she said in a rush. "Tiny and me, we can't figure how he's gonna get him out once he's all put back together."

"Probably has a plan, just playing his cards close to the chest." Marcel eyed Donut and she dodged his look. "I'll be off to Montreal for a few days," he said.

"Have a good trip." Donut got up and climbed down off the porch. "Gotta go. Late for school, like you said."

"I'll see you when I get back, yes?"

"Sure thing."

Lafayette and Rochambeau followed her down Marcel's long track to the main road. "Puppies, he knew something was up, but Marcel'd never dig around for answers a person didn't want to hand over." Donut stood between the puddles, catching her breath. "I know it's a crummy thing to do. But I've got no choice. I'm going to borrow Chanticleer, just for a little while."

They wagged their tails in unison, and she gave them each a pat on the head. When a dog wagged his tail, a person knew for absolute certain his happiness was the truth. Smiles could lie. Aunt Agnes's smile was canned peaches.

Donut hiked back to Slapp Hill Road and lugged her bags and fishing rod down the path to Dog Pond. The wind was blowing hard, kicking up waves and a cold spray of water off the rocks. She knew she should just haul her gear through the woods to the cabin. The *Nehi* wasn't built for this kind of weather. But she couldn't leave it behind. Her pops' boat would keep her safe. She was sure of it.

She tramped through the brush to the *Nehi*, unfolded it, secured the latches, lay the paddles inside, and wrestled it down to the shore. Once she had the boat bobbing in the shallow water she stowed her gear in the bow and climbed in without much fuss, except for her boots taking on some pond water.

The waves pushed her into shore, and the *Nehi* scraped up on the rocks. Donut centered herself on the middle bench seat, jammed her paddle into the mud, and got herself free. On the far shore, Chanticleer peeked out of the trees at her, waiting. She was doing it. She was on her way. Off into the unknown like Nellie Bly starting out on her race around the world. Donut laughed out loud at the thought. Dog Pond was just a little thing compared to the oceans of the world. But it was plenty big for now.

It was rough going. The bow of the tin boat reared up over every wave and slapped back down into the trough that followed, kicking up an icy spray. Donut paddled hard and found some kind of wild rhythm. In the center of Dog Pond, the *Nehi* tipped and bucked in the dark water over the deep spot.

"It's not like I couldn't swim to shore if I sunk," she said to her gear in the bow of the boat.

Donut glanced down at her boots, tied up in double

knots. She should have untied them before setting off, just in case. If the *Nehi* sank they'd fill with water, drag her right down to the bottom.

She set the paddle across her lap and untied her boot-laces, fumbling around as the boat rocked. A gust of wind caught the *Nehi* broadside. It spun around, bouncing and tipping. Donut gripped her paddle and aimed for Chanticleer, straight into the wind. She was scared now, and soaked with icy water.

"Don't think about it," she said. "You're almost there."

Past the deep spot, the wind let up some, blocked by the hills along the shore. The little boat was easier to handle. Donut paddled slower; her shoulders ached.

If the *Nehi* sank out from under her now she'd make it to shore, but all her supplies would vanish into the murky darkness. Schools of perch would nibble at her apples, gobble up the waterlogged crackers. The tins would take a while to rust through—maybe next winter the bottom-feeders would have a fish dinner when the headless sardines escaped their prison cells.

"Easy there, *Nehi*," Donut whispered. She could see Marcel's camp clearly now. A one-room shack with a shingled roof. The hillside was thick with cedars, shadowy and cold.

She pushed forward and entered the inlet below a rocky trail leading up to Chanticleer. The *Nehi* scraped against the bottom until the bow was stuck on solid ground. She'd made it. All she had to do now was ease one leg over and get the rest of herself out.

Donut sat in her boat in the shadow of the forest and didn't move. She hadn't expected the darkness of it, or the falling-down look of Chanticleer up close. She hadn't expected the all-aloneness of it, with time slowed down to a trickle. But she wasn't going to sit in the boat like a scared little rabbit until the sun went down.

Donut stowed her paddle and swung her leg over the side. Cold pond water filled her boot and she sucked in a sharp breath at the shock of it. She was half in and half out and the *Nehi* tipped. She held the sides, edged her weight onto her wet foot, swung her dry leg up, and set her other foot in the water. Her feet slid on the slippery rocks, slid right out from under her, and she fell on both knees in the cold water. The *Nehi* got free of the rocks with her pushing on the side and started drifting away from shore.

"No, no. Come back," she called to her tin boat.

Donut pushed on the bottom with her hands and managed to stand. Weighed down now by all the water in her boots, she slogged out to sea after the *Nehi*. Her movements kicked up some waves, driving the tin boat farther out, but Donut caught hold of the bow and dug inside for the painter. Holding tight to the rope, she navigated through the rocky shallows and stepped up onshore.

14

The sun hadn't yet made it over the hill, leaving Marcel's cabin perched in shadow. Donut shivered, soggy with pond water. The breeze got her teeth jammering.

"Stop. Just stop all this quaking and trembling," she said to herself.

Fugitives had to be tough—live off grubs and rats roasted over a fire, beat off mountain lions with a tree branch, build a log house with just an ax and a coil of rope. She wasn't going to be some whimpering castaway.

Donut sat on a rock and dumped the water out of her boots. She hauled the *Nehi* up onshore and carted her duffel up the rocky trail to the cabin. The rough pine door to Chanticleer was stuck fast. She gave it a good kick and it swung open. A rain of dead leaves and sticks dropped down on her head from the eaves.

Donut stepped inside. Chanticleer had been taken over by dust and cobwebs. The small table and two wooden chairs by the window were woven together with spiderwebs. Even in the dim light she could see that the blue ticking on the mattresses barely held the horsehair stuffing together. Marcel hadn't been here in years.

Donut stood just inside the doorway, her book bag slung over her shoulder. Water dripped from her coat and boots onto the rough wood floor. It was going to be just her, all alone in this gloomy place for days and days. With the thought of it, her courage trickled away. She pulled in a big gulp of air, straightened up, and stamped her foot to knock the jitters out of herself. Dust and grit sprinkled down from the ceiling.

"First things first. Get the fire going."

She dragged her duffel into the cabin, dug out the matches, and built up paper and kindling and a few logs in the woodstove. It caught easily. The fire snapped and roared, breaking the silence.

She got out of her wet dress, pulled on dry clothes, and sat up close to the woodstove. The cabin was giving up its chill and a scritch-scratch started up behind the kitchen shelves. Chanticleer's mice were probably thrilled with the warmth, wiggling their tails in the hopes of a few odd crumbs dropped on the floor by their new roommate.

Left empty so long, Marcel's cabin had gotten all hollowed out. Her house on Slapp Hill would hollow out, too, if she was gone. Spiders and mice would move right in.

Donut grabbed hold of her wet boots and pulled them on. "You're not gonna get your way, Aunt Agnes. Not ever."

She stomped down the trail to fill a bucket with pond water. Back in the cabin Donut set a pot of water to boil on the woodstove. The blue blankets in the old wooden trunk smelled musty and forgotten. She carried them outside and hung them over a low branch to air out.

By the time the sun had made it over the hill she had scrubbed and swept Chanticleer clean—as clean as a rickety old cabin could get.

She sat at the table and ate her lunch while she watched a pair of wood ducks in the little cove where she'd landed the *Nehi*. The cheese and apple and crackers tasted especially good here in her hideout now that she'd settled in.

Behind her the door swung open and banged into the wall. She jumped.

Tiny filled the doorway, trying to catch his breath.

Donut got up from her chair. "You scared me," she said. "Barging in like that."

"What do you think you're doing?" Tiny glared at her.

She glared back. "I've run away."

"Without telling me?" He was yelling now. "You came over here in that stupid boat, too. It was gone. I thought you'd drowned."

"It's not a stupid boat."

"No, you're right. That boat's a real ace. You're the stupid one."

"Shut up, Tiny."

"No, I'm not shutting up. You're a real stinker, you know. Some friend."

"I couldn't tell you."

"Why not?"

"You're not a good liar. Can't bluff at poker. They'd be after you to turn me over. If Aunt Agnes got you alone you'd tell her everything. You know you would. And I'm not a stinker."

"Swell. You're not dead, either. So I'm leaving."

"Go ahead. See if I care." Donut plunked down in her chair.

Tiny turned and left the cabin. Donut got up and ran to the door. "You couldn't tell a lie to save your life!" she yelled.

He was halfway down the slope to the trail and didn't turn around. The not turning around put her in a panic. "Tiny," she called.

But he kept going and disappeared at the bend in the trail.

Donut scrubbed at her face, put a stop to any tears. Tiny knowing she was here would have made the alone part not so bad. But now with her being a stinker and not admitting it and Tiny mad at her, the alone part was going to be worse than ever.

She sat back down in her chair by the stove. She'd run away and lost her best friend. She should load all her gear back in the *Nehi*, go home, and find Tiny, keep saying she was sorry until he forgave her. But she couldn't or she'd end up in Boston. She'd made a mess of things.

"Can't fix it," she said to herself.

Donut kicked off her slippers and pulled her wet boots on. Bundled up in her not-quite-dry coat, she got herself outside.

The trail around the pond wove through cedars and the boggy wet. Brilliant green skunk cabbage shoots dotted the forest floor alongside moss-covered boulders that the cedars had wrapped up tight with dark roots. She jumped a creek and sank a little in the muck, found deer tracks and Tiny's boot prints.

"I'm sorry," she whispered to his tracks in the mud.

When she got to the old maple she stopped. A wood-pecker had dug out another hollow in the trunk and a large branch had fallen and opened up a window to the sky. This was where they'd turned to get to their fishing rock, her pops and her, in the summer, the woods full of birds.

The granite outcropping was like a giant's foot poking its toes into the pond. "How about a trip to the big toe?"

he'd say, and her pops would drag out his straw hat with the red band around it. They'd sit on the big toe, hang their legs down off the edge, their fishing lines in the water below.

She reached up and laid her hand flat on the crusty bark of the old maple. It just kept going—woodpeckers chipping out holes, the wind blowing off branches. With trees it was all about luck. Wherever they took root, that was it—in the shadows or a wet spot, wherever an animal or the wind carried the seed, the start of them.

This old maple had landed in a lucky spot and brought the whole forest to itself. How many birds had it raised up in nests tucked in the high branches? For years and years, insects had chewed at its leaves and squirrels had scrabbled up the trunk to find a safe hiding spot.

Donut sat in a hollow in the roots of the tree, leaned against it, willing it to talk to her, whisper stories of summer nights, tell of the time a fox might have curled up right here and slept, its belly full of chokecherries, baby birds, and wild raspberries.

This old tree remembered her pops, his beat-up straw hat with the red band. This old tree had seen him smile down at her and put his hand on her shoulder as they walked under its branches, out to their fishing spot on Dog Pond.

Donut kicked at one of the great roots. She was such a

sad little bunny, all crunched up in a huddle by this broken-down tree on the very first day of her being a runaway. Talking trees. It was a wonder she'd made it to Chanticleer in the first place.

She hiked back to the cabin, sloshing through the mud, annoyed at the crows and their warnings as she approached.

"What do you think I'm gonna do, you old cranks?"

They kept at it, cawing and cackling, and Donut wished she had a throwing arm like Tiny's.

And she wished she hadn't been such a lousy friend.

At the cabin, she carried in the bedding and made up the bottom bunk bed. She lugged in a few loads of half-rotted firewood from the stack outside.

She heated some canned milk on the woodstove and made herself a mug of Ovaltine. Drinking it slowly, she looked out at the pond. The wood ducks were gone. But the mice in the walls were doing their scritch-scratch over by the counter and she was glad for the company. A log in the stove dropped with a loud clunk.

What with getting soaked through and running away and having a full-out fight with her best friend, Donut was so tired she couldn't keep her eyes open. It was still light outside, but she didn't care. Still in her clothes she climbed into her bunk, pulled the covers up, and fell asleep.

Donut woke in the cold dark, sat up straight, bumping her head on the top bunk. The mice raced for cover.

"It's okay," she said. "Just me."

Her voice sounded small and tinny in the pitch-dark. Donut stumbled around, found the matches, and lit the lantern. She sat down in her chair and ate an apple for dinner. Since she was in charge of herself now, she could stay up as late as she wanted. She could light up a pipe, drink a bottle of hooch, do any darn thing she pleased. But all she wanted to do was crawl back into bed.

She set an apple crate on its side by her bunk and on top of that she put a candle in a tin cup, a box of matches, and the picture of her pops and her in the silver frame. After she made a trip to the outhouse she changed into her night-clothes, blew out the candle, and climbed in under the scratchy blankets.

Lying there, it seemed especially dark in the cabin. And there were noises—a bump on the roof, a high-pitched screech in the woods, the creaking of branches in the wind. The stillness inside the cabin made the noises outside louder. And she was alone.

Another bump on the roof. A string of bumps, like foot-steps. What was up there? She'd heard stories of fisher cats. They were real mean when they got cornered. Mr. Hollis had said when he was a boy a fisher cat got into the family chicken coop and killed every last hen. He'd found six of them stashed on a high branch of a beech tree, their necks broken.

It started up again. Right over her head. Donut fumbled with the matches and lit the candle. The footsteps stopped. She got up, ran over to the woodstove, and grabbed hold of the iron poker. Laying her weapon on the floor by the bed, she got back under the covers.

Donut shivered, eyes wide in the dark. Sam had said that no one had seen a fisher cat in Vermont for years and years. All trapped out for their fur. But that didn't mean for certain that one hadn't wandered down from Canada, climbed up on the roof of Chanticleer, and was trying to figure out a way to get inside. She'd been plenty scared before—chased by dogs, stuck up a pine tree with no idea how to climb back down—but she'd never been this all-alone scared.

Whatever was stomping around on the roof was done stomping. She tried closing her eyes, but closing them seemed to pull the scariness outside the cabin right inside. At least the clouds had moved off and moonlight poured in through the window. Donut leaned over and blew out the candle. Just a minute later she heard a hooting sort of bark. Very loud and close, down by the water. She lay there under the covers, listening.

She'd never heard a bear hoot, but she figured this was it. Tiny'd described it, and so had Pudge. Like an owl, but not an owl. Like a dog, but not a dog. It had a heft to it, but didn't really sound bearlike.

She lay still and listened. There were two of them. Calling back and forth across Dog Pond. One was far away and sounded kind of sad. She'd seen a bear last year, up a tree, feeding on beechnuts in the woods out by the Patoines' lower field.

Donut got out of bed, pulled her slippers on, and crept over to the window. She gazed out at the pond, washed in moonlight. The bear was down by the water's edge, his head lifted up, snout pointing toward the opposite shore. He hooted right then, while she stood in her slippers in the moonlit cabin. His friend across the way hooted back, a longer call with a short break, then a quick bark at the end of it.

The bear down by the shore stood. He stood up on his hind legs and stared out over the water. He waited. Donut looked out over the pond and waited, too. The call came, a single hoot from far away. The bear dropped back down on all four legs and walked off into the woods in the direction of the old maple tree. She wondered what a bear meeting would be like. A rough-and-tumble if they were both male? Maybe a shy lumbering through the woods if they were a mated pair.

The stove rumbled and kicked out heat. Donut climbed back into bed, yanked her mother's sleeping cap down over her ears. She wasn't scared of the bears. She wouldn't want to meet up on the trail or in a berry patch in August, but her bears were watching the woods. Keeping an eye on things. Donut pulled the covers up tight. Not quite so alone in the dark now, she fell asleep, half listening to a mouse chewing on what she figured was one of her crackers on the shelf.

15

That first morning Donut discovered the evidence of more than one mouse on the shelves where she'd stored her food. Crackers had been dragged out of the paper sack and nibbled at in a dark corner. The skin of one apple was ragged and the white fruit underneath gnawed with small teeth. She cleaned up the mouse droppings and moved all her food into the trunk by her bed.

"There's not enough to share with you. But you can have the crumbs," she said to the mice in the walls and under the floorboards.

After breakfast Donut got dressed, stuffed the mouse-chewed apple into her coat pocket, and walked down to the pond to fetch a bucket of water. There were tracks in the mud among the rocks on the shore—big bear tracks, wide and solid, with the toe prints all in a row. Donut laid her hand flat, fingers spread inside a track, and pressed down, touching her moonlight bear. She set the apple on a flat rock—a gift.

When she turned to pick up the bucket she noticed the spot under the cedar on the edge of the cove was empty. The *Nehi* was gone. Donut ran as best she could over the rocks and mud until she got around the spit of land that blocked her view. Two boys were in her boat on the far northern shore, zigzagging around, splashing each other with the paddles.

She could hear their hollering now, and there was no mistaking who the thieves were, what with the cuss words getting thrown around and the red-and-black-checked caps they both wore.

"Wally Ducharme, you weasel, bring my boat back," she yelled.

Wally and his little brother, Pete, both turned and started laughing.

"I mean it," said Donut. "You'll be the sorriest brothers in Caledonia County if you don't get back here."

They headed toward her, rocking the boat with uneven paddling.

"That you, Donut?" said Wally. He stood up in the stern and the *Nehi* tipped way over to the right.

"Sit down, you knucklehead," said Donut, clenching her fists.

Pete laughed. Wally sat back down and whacked his brother on the shoulder with his paddle. Pete swung round and whacked Wally. The boat rocked.

They got about twenty feet from shore, stopped paddling, and sat in the *Nehi*, both grinning, knowing full well that she couldn't grab hold of them and wring their scrawny necks.

"This where you're hidin' out?" asked Wally.

"What's it to you?" said Donut.

"Whole town knows you gave that aunt of yours the slip."

"Marcel know you're using his camp?" asked Pete, leaning over the side of the boat with his hand in the water.

"What business is it of yours?"

"Boy, oh boy, we ever ran off, wouldn't be able to sit down for a week," said Wally, shaking his head. "You're gonna catch it when they find you."

They were trouble. The worst kind of trouble. Miss Beebe'd worn out a couple of rulers on these two on account of them being real stinkers—tripping little kids, stealing lunches and nickels. Last winter they'd loaded the woodstove in the schoolroom with firecrackers, and when the string of kabooms went off it about gave Miss Beebe apoplexy. Too dumb to look innocent, they were the only ones laughing and got a good whack from her and a tanning from their dad when he found out.

"I need that boat," said Donut.

"Did you hear that, Pete? She needs her boat," said Wally.

Donut knew she had to calm down. Getting her all riled up was way too much fun for these two. She found a large rock close to shore and sat down all peaceful.

"Gee, boys, I sure hope you're not gonna squeal on me to Ernie or anyone else."

Wally got a disgusted look on his face. "We ain't squealers. And besides, you've done pretty good, for a girl, sneaking off like that."

"And we're just borrowing your boat," said Pete.

"It's my pops' boat. Kind of tippy. Don't want you to drown even if you did steal it. I gotta have it handy 'cause I might need to make a quick getaway."

"Not much of a getaway, stuck paddling around in this puddle," said Wally.

Things had gotten sort of friendly. Donut grinned. They grinned back and Pete smacked the water with his paddle. The Ducharme boys were trouble, but they had no liking for grown-ups and rules. Their dad snapped orders like he was spitting tacks, and they hopped to it. He was hard on his animals, too.

"Listen, my aunt's gonna haul me off to Boston. I've got to hold out here until she gives up and leaves. I need your help."

"Well, sure. We could stand guard. Set up snares," said Wally.

"Thanks for the offer, but what I really need is for you two to swear you won't tell a soul where I am."

Wally nudged Pete and they paddled into shore alongside the rock where Donut was sitting. He studied her for a minute, spit in his hand, and offered it up. Donut spit in her own hand, reached across the water, and they shook. Pete did the same.

"Meet you over by the camp," said Wally, pushing off from the rock with his paddle.

Donut hiked back, and she and Wally carried the *Nehi* up over the rocks, flipped it over, and set it under the cedar tree.

"So why aren't you two in school?" said Donut.

"No reason."

"You're gonna catch it from Miss Beebe."

"Get whacked with her ruler plenty when we're there. What's the difference?"

"Yeah, what's the difference," said Pete.

"That's true." Donut marveled at the logic of it.

"Okay. Got things to do," said Wally. He pulled his slingshot out of his back pocket.

"Yeah, stuff to do," said Pete.

"Thanks for staying quiet," said Donut.

She watched them disappear into the woods and felt kind of bad for the squirrels along the trail since Wally could knock a nickel off a post with that slingshot of his. The Ducharme boys weren't all bad when they weren't caged up in the schoolhouse. She filled her water bucket and climbed back up the trail to the cabin.

The rest of the morning she spent on the map of South Dakota out of respect for Teddy Roosevelt. There were a lot of buttes—Thunder Butte, Red Butte, Slim Butte. They were like giant tree stumps or Lincoln's top hat, but jagged and rocky, not like the soft, green hills in Vermont. She'd like to see one of them up close one day.

Donut had sardines and crackers for lunch, cleaned up, and sat back down at the table. This running away business was going to bore the teeth out of her head. The cabin was scrubbed raw, probably cleaner than it'd been in years, and she'd hauled enough wood inside to last a week. How could Aunt Agnes stand it, sitting in the parlor all day with no company, no nothing to keep her occupied except knitting those blasted socks?

Donut pulled her coat on, walked down to the shore, and collected about twenty skipping stones—flat and round, just the right size. She stood on a rock close to the water and practiced her side-arm throw. She got six skips out of her last stone and climbed down for more.

"Thought you'd be studying your atlas," said Tiny from up by the trail. "You should have the whole thing down cold with all this time on your hands."

Donut grinned at him. He'd come back. It was better than good to see him. The joy of it about knocked her off her feet. "Finished with geography for now," she said. "Time moves so slow out here. If I had a clock it would stop ticking."

"Well," said Tiny, "clocks are ticking along everywhere else, and I've got news."

Inside Chanticleer she set a pan of milk on the stove to warm while Tiny watched from a chair at the table. She was so glad he was sitting there in the cabin she didn't much care what the news was, good or bad.

"I'm really sorry, Tiny."

He frowned. "You oughta be."

"But how'd you find me yesterday?"

"You weren't at the bridge. I knocked on the door and your aunt said you'd left already. You weren't in the schoolyard. Figured you were playing hooky, gone fishing. Got up here and the boat was gone. Thought you'd drowned. Saw the smoke at Marcel's here. Took the path, ran the whole way."

"Sorry I scared you. Really."

"But why'd you do it? You've stirred up the whole village."

"The supper didn't work. Sam tried, even told her I could live with him, but she turned him down flat. I had to run away. Had no choice."

Tiny shook his head. "She's gonna wait you out, you know."

"I know, but maybe she'll see what a load of trouble I'm gonna be and let me stay with Sam."

"Might work," said Tiny. He punched her on the arm, kind of hard. "But why didn't you tell me?"

"Aunt Agnes gets you all twitchy, and you're already an awful liar. You really are. You just don't have the face for it."

"I can lie when I've got to. Does Marcel know you're here?"

"Not exactly."

Tiny didn't say anything. Just sat in his chair, bumping one knee up and down, fingering a throwing stone in his big fist.

"What?" she said.

"First off, you shouldn't be using his camp without asking. And you've got everyone worried—Sam, my folks, the Mayos, Miss Beebe. Ernie's Ford was parked at your house this morning."

"Aunt Agnes told them, right? Told them I left a note, that I didn't drown or get lost in the woods?"

"Yeah, they know you ran, but that doesn't mean they're not gonna worry."

"I know, okay. I know."

Donut stood and kept her back to Tiny as she poured hot milk out of the saucepan into two mugs and stirred in the Ovaltine. She handed Tiny his mug and sat down with hers.

"Got you yesterday's *Gazette* out of Sam's wood box." He pulled the wrinkled newspaper out of his back pocket and set it on the table.

She was glad to have Tiny sitting there, but it was tough being a fugitive, so close to home, with everyone else's feelings getting tangled up in hers. A clean break would have been a whole lot easier. Across Lake Champlain, in some deserted camp in the Adirondacks, she would have been totally, completely alone and probably scared silly day and night, but it would have been way simpler.

Donut gazed out at Dog Pond. She kicked the table leg and their mugs of Ovaltine jumped and slopped over.

"You can tell them, Tiny. Sam and the rest. Don't tell them where I'm hiding, just that you've seen me and I'm fine. But not Ernie. If he gets wind of it Mr. Hollis'll be tacking my picture up next to the ten-most-wanted list at the post office."

"Nobody tells Ernie anything. He'll just keep driving round in circles."

They both laughed. But Tiny's laugh was a kind of a smothered laugh.

"How's Winnie?"

He was quiet for a while. Sipped at his Ovaltine. "She's not eating much of anything."

"Oh, Tiny. That's not good."

He stared down at his boots. Donut reached across the table and gripped his arm. He looked up at her.

"I'm some kind of fool to care so much for a damn cow."

"But she's Winnie."

"Yeah." He stood up and pulled on his boots and coat. "Got to get back."

Standing right outside the door he gave her a serious look, eyebrows hunched up. "I won't tell where you are even if the whole lot of 'em gangs up on me. I promise."

"Thanks, and give Winnie a scratch behind the ears for me. I'm really sorry I was such a louse."

He turned and headed for the trail at a good clip.

Just then, Donut realized she'd forgotten to tell Tiny about the bears.

16

Her second night in Chanticleer Donut lay still under the blankets doing her best to fall asleep. She steadied her breathing, tried to ignore the scampering of the mice. Alone in the dark cabin, the night noises were so much closer— the creak of wood, movement in the forest, the squawk of a bird awakened by some unknown night animal. Something scraped against the back wall of the cabin and Donut sat up and stared into the dark.

And then the bears began their hooting barks. Back and forth across Dog Pond. The same double call, over and over. It was sad, really, that call. Hadn't they found each other last night? It was dark as pitch, with clouds blocking the moon, so Donut lay back down in her warm bed and listened.

Would her bear find the apple? Wonder where it had come from? She could invite him in for a cup of Ovaltine. He could sit in Tiny's chair at the table. Tell her of the forest—of climbing apple trees, raiding beehives, and his dreams in winter while he slept in some cave or great hole dug into the side of a hill. Like Badger in *The Wind in the Willows*, which her pops had read aloud to her, her bear would be dignified, his home well appointed with easy chairs and a very large feather bed.

At dawn, Donut woke to a steady rain pounding on the roof. The cabin was dark and cold. She got up shivering, built a fire in the stove, and climbed back into bed.

"This just beats all," she said, rolling over and kicking at the covers.

A cold rain would keep her cooped up all day. Tiny probably wouldn't come, what with the added work of the cows in the barn, the slog through the mud to the cabin, and Winnie.

She finally had to get out of bed to use the outhouse. And no matter the rain, she had to check on the apple. With her hat pulled down over her ears Donut walked down to the shore. The apple was gone and fresh bear tracks were everywhere, filled up with rainwater—bear puddles. She'd leave a fresh snack for him.

"Would you like cheese? Or maybe sardines?"

She knew she shouldn't be feeding her bear, drawing him to the cabin. He was a bear, after all, with claws and teeth, and used to getting his own way. But she wasn't scared of this particular bear.

Donut slipped and slid her way back up the trail and settled down at the table with the *Gazette*. She read it straight through—every news flash, article, advertisement, and two pages of personals. A freight train had derailed in Maryland and carloads of Florida oranges had rolled down a hillside. What a sight that must have been.

Done with the paper, she stared out the window at the rain. The cabin would float away soon. The pond would rise and rise. She'd fill a sack with food and float off in the *Nehi*, drift south all the way to Maryland, where oranges would be bobbing in the floodwaters. Easy pickings. She'd fill the boat and paddle north as the water receded.

The rain kept on all day. At sunset Tiny still hadn't come. Donut opened her last can of sardines, laid half of them out on a metal pie pan, and carried her offering down to the shore. The bear tracks were blurred by the rain, their edges worn down. She set the pie tin on the flat rock.

Back inside, she sat at the table and watched the shore. There was no movement, no wind. She heard the scribble-scrabble of a mouse and turned slowly toward the sound. He was on the counter, a deer mouse with a notch in his left ear, on the top edge—a near miss. He held a cracker crumb in his front paws, nibbled at it, turned the crumb over and nibbled some more.

"You're awful daring," she whispered.

The mouse froze, twitched his whiskers. What did they tell him, those whiskers? He relaxed and continued nibbling. Donut watched the movement of his delicate fingers. The crumb gone, the notch-eared mouse disappeared behind the counter.

It was dark now, and the rain had eased up a little. She ate the rest of the sardines with crackers and a mug of Ovaltine. That was the end of the milk. Cheese and apples and crackers were all she had left for food. If the blasted rain would let up she'd go fishing tomorrow and have a proper dinner.

It was early still, but Donut cleaned up and went to bed. Being a runaway was dull as ditchwater. She was still a little scared when she blew out the candle, but the scariness of the night noises and dark in the cabin were familiar now. Besides, her bear was probably nearby, standing guard while he ate his fish dinner.

Donut woke to still more rain. Down on the shore a couple of blue jays had dumped the pie tin into the mud and were dickering over the sardines.

All day she sat in the cabin. All day it rained.

How did Robinson Crusoe do it, all this peace and quiet? He waited for years and years for a ship to appear on the horizon. If she got shipwrecked, she'd build a raft straight-away and go to sea. Drifting toward the world was better than getting old, waiting politely for it to arrive.

The rain started to let up in the late afternoon. Donut sat at the table studying the map of North Dakota.

The cabin door opened behind her.

"Just sittin' there like the queen of Sheba." Tiny set down a sack by the door. "And you're dry as a chip."

She laughed at the sight of him—a drowned rat with a large puddle already forming under him from the drip-drip of his boots and coat.

"It's not funny. I'm soaked through."

Tiny wrestled himself out of his coat and muddy boots and set a milk can on the table. He grabbed his chair and plunked down close to the stove. Steam rose off his wet shirt and hair and socks.

"I sure am glad to see you," she said. "And fresh milk, thanks."

She filled the saucepan, set it on the stove, and pulled up a chair next to him.

"There's more," said Tiny, reaching his stocking feet out toward the fire.

He pulled a waxed-paper package out of his sack and handed it to her.

She knew right away what it was. She could have smelled Mrs. Lamphere's gingersnaps a mile off.

"I was in the store and Mrs. Stratton pulled them out from under the counter. 'We know you know where she is,' she says. 'And Gladys made this batch up special for you to take to our young runaway.'"

"What did you say? You didn't let on where I was, did you?"

"No. And she never asked." Tiny started pulling other things out of the sack. "A Hershey bar from the Barclay boys. Pudge sent along a deck of cards. Doris says hi, and she sent this brand-new tablet. Said you should write down your adventures and sell 'em to the *Saturday Evening Post*."

"I can't believe it."

"Sam sent on the latest *Gazette* and your taxidermy tools."

Tiny kept hauling things out of the sack. An old compass from Artie Bellevance, mittens from Tiny's mom, a jug of maple syrup from Beryl. Donut laughed—Mr. Hollis at the post office had sent her an orange.

They were all on her side. She hadn't really run away, what with the bits of everyone now stacked up on the table.

"What about Aunt Agnes?"

"Don't know. I duck past your house pretty fast. And been steering clear of Ernie."

Donut fixed mugs of Ovaltine for herself and Tiny and unwrapped the gingersnaps. He was quiet, staring out the window.

"How's Winnie?"

Tiny's shoulders sagged.

"Poorly," he said, not looking at her. "Leg won't bear any weight. We're gonna have to put her down."

"Oh, Tiny."

"She's suffering. Ribs are showing."

"There's no way to fix it? Put a splint on her leg? Keep her in the stall 'til it heals?"

"She doesn't understand what's happened, just keeps trying to get up, move around."

"I'm so sorry, Tiny."

"Winnie's a good girl."

They sat at the table drinking Ovaltine and eating gingersnaps and the rain started up again, drumming on the roof. There wasn't anything Donut could say to make it easier for Tiny. That was one thing she knew for sure. Everyone had tried for words to say when her pops had died, and they always just fumbled around, making a mess of it. Sometimes a person could stand up to the sadness better without words stirring it up. She tried her best to sit still with Tiny and his sorrow.

After a bit he set his empty mug down on the table. "So what's your plan?"

"Don't really have one besides hiding out here."

"Sooner than later your auntie's gonna flush you out."

Aunt Agnes. She was the only one in Cobden besides

Ernie who was in the dark. Aunt Agnes, sitting in her wing-back chair, was more alone than Donut was hiding out in Chanticleer. She picked up another gingersnap and chewed at it. If Aunt Agnes was lonely, she could always get on the train and go back to Boston.

17

Sunday morning Donut woke up to cloudy skies but no rain. It was time to catch some perch or maybe even a lake trout if she was lucky. Out by the woodpile she dug up some worms and stuck them in a sardine can. She dragged the *Nehi* down to the water and it scraped something awful on the rocks when she slid around in the slippery stretches of mud.

With no wind to speak of, she paddled quickly out to the middle of Dog Pond. Floating over the deep spot, she gripped the paddle tight. The darkness below, the not knowing what was down there, was like the emptiness of Ichabod's eye sockets.

It was chilly and the worm didn't wiggle much when Donut stuck it on the hook. There was water in the bottom of the boat. Her boots were getting soggy. The lead weight pulled the line down a good ways until it went slack. She reeled in a few feet and waited. The water in the bottom of the *Nehi* seemed to be getting deeper. It was sloshing around now when she moved on her seat.

Donut set the end of the fishing rod down and made a close inspection of the hull. Nothing. She turned and checked the stern. Hidden under the bench seat, there was a hole in the boat. A good-sized hole, with bits of metal, all jagged, sticking up around it. The boat was filling up fast.

Donut yanked her hat off, tried to stuff it in the hole, getting a sizable cut on her thumb in the process. The water in the boat was up to her seat now and had taken on a pinkish tone from the blood dripping down her hand.

She tried to paddle but the *Nehi* was so weighed down with water it wouldn't budge. Donut twisted around, jammed her boot down over the hole, but the metal sticking up kept her from sealing it.

It was all happening so fast. Her pops' boat was sinking. She shouldn't have dragged it over the rocks.

"Get your boots off!"

Her boots would drag her, feet first, down to the bottom of Dog Pond along with this stupid tin bucket. Donut fumbled in the water in the boat, untied the laces, and pulled her boots off. She tied them together and strung them around her neck.

The sardine can with the worms in it bobbed around in

the boat, not leaking one bit. A better design than her pops had come up with. Donut grabbed it.

"Stupid tin can!" she hollered, and threw it far out over Dog Pond.

Right then, with a few inches of boat left, with her sitting in freezing pond water, the line took off from her rod. She'd caught a fish. She grabbed the pole and the line zipped out.

With her boots around her neck and a fish on the line, the boat sank out from under her. With the shock of the icy cold, she let go of the fishing rod. Thrashing her arms around, she got her head above water. Below her she could just make out the *Nehi*. It rolled over and cut down into the deep like a silver whale.

Donut sank again, her head underwater. She was so cold and had so much weight on her with her coat and clothes and boots around her neck, she just might drown. She swung her arms, got her head out of the water once again and twirled around until she located Chanticleer on the hillside. She could swim it easy in the summer, but this was altogether different.

She started in dog-paddling, stirred up a froth with her panic, inched forward with the boots dangling from her neck, heavy as two boulders. She wasn't giving them up. She'd already lost her fishing rod, the fish on the hook— and the *Nehi*.

Donut kicked and paddled. She kicked her feet, searching for the bottom, the eelgrass, rocks, mud. Nothing. She kept paddling. Her head ached with the cold. She kept kicking, her eyes on Chanticleer.

Her toe brushed the rocky bottom and she flailed around until she was standing with just her head poking up out of the water.

"Don't stop," she sputtered.

She'd freeze up solid if she stopped. She'd give up if she stopped. Donut leaned forward, pushed off the bottom with her feet, paddled with her hands.

The climbing up on shore part was colder than the being in the water part. Donut pulled her boots off her neck and dropped them next to the pie tin on the rocks. Her feet were so cold, putting weight on them stabbed at her toes and heels. She slipped and slid up the trail to Chanticleer.

Inside the cabin, she pulled off her wet clothes and wrapped herself up in one of the wool blankets on her bed. She loaded wood into the stove, got it roaring hot. The stovepipe glowed pink and she sat up close to the heat, shivering and shaking and cussing.

She'd picked up loads of cuss words from André and Marcel and her pops when they hadn't thought she was listening. She let them loose now. A whole string of foul words. She could see why they did it. It helped a whole lot to cuss.

The *Nehi* was gone. Sunk. If she'd been paying attention she would have wondered about the water coming in long before she'd gotten all the way out to the deep spot. She would have had time to paddle back to shore. To save her pops' boat. Which had turned out to not be so sturdy after all. He wouldn't ever have made his fortune on the foolish thing, like he'd kept saying. People would have drowned left and right in rivers and lakes and ponds from coast to coast.

As she warmed up and the shivering slowed down Donut got even madder. At the whole stinking world. The flat tire. The long skid and roll and him flying. Flying. And on top of her pops being dead, the whole running away idea was stupid. Aunt Agnes had made up her mind. She wasn't going to just pick up and leave Donut to Sam. She'd sit in that parlor knitting her ugly socks and wait. She was old. Old people were patient. Had nothing better to do. And the *Nehi* was gone. A piece of her pops—not his cleverest invention, but still, his boat, just sitting there on the bottom of Dog Pond, forever.

And she'd caught a fish, too. And it had gotten away, along with her fishing rod. All of it. Gone. And it was going to take days for her clothes to dry out.

Donut couldn't decide if she was going to cry or bust up the furniture. Either way, it wouldn't change anything. The *Nehi* was gone and her pops was dead.

18

Donut sat for a long time, wrapped up in the scratchy wool blanket in front of the woodstove, her wet clothes in a heap on the floor. She would have stayed there forever, cussing and mumbling about the rotten hand she got dealt from day one, but she had to use the outhouse.

She pulled on dry socks and her nightclothes. It wasn't even dark yet, but she didn't care. Her slippers got muddy on the trip to the outhouse, but she stopped and looked out over the pond. The sun was setting and the sky was a washed-out blue. There was no sign of the *Nehi*. No ripples or any hint at all. Her boat was just swallowed up.

Back inside Chanticleer, Donut lit the lamp and made herself a cup of Ovaltine. She studied the heap of wet clothes by the door while she ate two gingersnaps. The wet mess could all just lie there. She blew out the lamp, and crawled into bed.

The mice woke her up. They were skittering around over by the table. Donut got out of bed and lit the lantern. Scurrying feet retreated into cracks and crevices.

They'd gotten into the gingersnaps and gnawed through the wrapper of the Hershey bar. Bits of paper were scattered about, and mouse droppings, too. There must have been a whole battalion of them eating the presents that Tiny had lugged through the mud.

"You little creeps!" she yelled.

Donut pulled down three rusty mousetraps she'd seen on the top shelf. It was all her fault, since she hadn't put the food away.

"Tough luck."

She baited the traps with ruined bits of her Hershey bar. One she put on the counter by the crack where the notch-eared mouse had disappeared earlier, and the other two she put along the floor against the wall, right where they liked to creep.

The moon was full-on bright and she could see her boots down by the shore. The bears were gone, along with the *Nehi*. And here she was, wide-awake in the middle of the night. She draped her coat over Tiny's chair by the stove and hung her other wet things over the woodpile. All of it had that pond smell, not fishy, but alive—an ancient, sad kind of smell.

Her atlas was open to the map of Louisiana. She traced the coastline with her finger. She should run away good and proper—board a steamer in New York Harbor, not go ashore until it docked in New Orleans. The sailors on board would teach her how to tie knots and drink rum. She'd eat hardtack and sing wicked sea chanteys. Everyone in Cobden would hear about the disappearance of the *Nehi*. They'd figure she'd drowned, have a big funeral. And because it was believed the fish in Dog Pond had eaten the dead eleven-year-old Dorothy Sedgewick, no one would ever again be entirely comfortable frying up a bucket of perch they'd caught in those waters.

Donut closed up her atlas and blew out the lantern. She sat at the table and gazed down at the water. Maybe her bear had found his way through the woods and around the pond to the far shore. Maybe he had no reason to call to the other bear now because they were together.

She lit the candle on the apple crate, picked up the photograph of her and her pops in the silver frame, and climbed into bed. In the photograph, he was wearing his army uniform from the Great War over in France.

She had on a white baby dress with smocking and ribbons and tiny stitches. The dress went down way past her toes and made it look like she could fly, not needing the use of her feet and legs. As she circled above her crib her pops would reach up for the ribbons, try to drag her back down to earth like the musclemen at the Lamoille County Fair pulling on the ropes to get the rainbow-striped hot-air balloon to behave.

In the photograph her pops sat a little stiff in his uniform, but he had a smile on his face and he was aiming it right at her, holding her in the crook of his elbow. Her pops had a smile that made a person want to twirl in a circle with arms wide.

Donut set the photograph in the silver frame back on the apple crate and blew out the candle. The missing her pops was a wave this time, an ache moving through her guts. Under the blankets, her eyes closed, she waited for it to ease. She knew now it would, because a person couldn't hurt like this for too long or they'd just die.

Donut crawled out of bed just before dawn the next morning. She pulled on her clothes and slippers and took a trip to the outhouse. Back in the cabin she reached for the can of Ovaltine and saw that the mousetrap on the counter was flipped over. A mouse tail poked out. She took a quick breath and picked the trap up by the edges. The metal bar held the body down tight and the tail drooped. It wasn't the notch-eared mouse. But still, she was sorry she'd killed it. The scritch-scratch of the mice in Chanticleer had kept her company. She lifted the bar off and slid the dead mouse onto the table.

"Hey, Donut. You in there?"

She turned. Someone was banging on the door.

"Tiny?"

The door swung open and Wally and Pete came trooping in. Wally held up her boots and Pete handed her the empty pie tin.

"Boat's gone. Didn't see it on the water, neither," said Wally.

"Thought you drowned," said Pete.

"Almost did," said Donut. She set her boots down by the woodstove.

"Tip over?" asked Wally.

"Nope. Sprung a leak. Boat sunk."

"Jeesh," said Pete.

"That's too bad," said Wally. "But hey, good thing you didn't drown 'cause we brought you breakfast."

"Bacon," said Pete.

"Ma won't miss it, just a small slab hanging way back in the smokehouse," said Wally, handing her a soot-covered end of bacon.

"Spring pig," said Pete.

"Thanks, boys," she said. "I'm running low on food."

"Got eggs, too."

Pete proudly pulled a handkerchief out of his coat pocket. It was yellow with yoke. Donut took it in two hands and opened it up on the counter.

"Three out of four's not bad," she said.

"I told you to keep 'em in your hat," said Wally.

"Hey, you know there's a dead mouse on the table?" said Pete holding it up by its tail.

Donut took the mouse, set it on the trunk, and got busy cutting up chunks of bacon with her jackknife. "Stick around for breakfast, why don't you."

She added wood to the stove and fried up the bacon and eggs in an old skillet. The smell made her stomach rumble. Wally and Pete inspected the cabin and settled at the table, Wally in Tiny's chair and Pete on an apple crate.

"That old stovepipe's gettin' kind of red-hot, ain't it?" said Wally.

"It's been cold with all the rain." Donut studied the pipe. It did look about ready to give out. She'd need to keep an eye on it.

"Anyway, it's a good hideout," said Wally. "Marcel know you're here? You never said."

Donut didn't answer. She busied herself serving up breakfast.

"Some dogs he's got," said Wally.

"Eat you alive," said Pete.

"Not if they know you," said Donut.

The three of them sat at the table and ate their bacon and eggs off three pie tins. She'd never seen the Ducharme boys so quiet.

Wally wiped the grease off his mouth with the back of his sleeve. "Took care of Ernie for a while."

Pete giggled.

"Jeez, boys, what'd you do?"

"Snuck out around midnight last night," said Wally. "Shoved a potato up the tailpipe of his old Ford. It'll kill the engine dead 'til he figures out what's wrong. If you need to make a quick getaway, he won't be on the road for a while."

Pete grinned, egg yolk on his chin.

Donut smiled. She couldn't help it. They were so proud to be fellow outlaws.

"Thanks, but lay off Ernie for a while. I don't want you getting into trouble 'cause of me."

"He can't prove a thing. Anyway, gotta get to school. Miss Beebe's waiting with her ruler." Wally stood. Pete jumped up.

"Great breakfast," said Donut.

She watched from the doorway until the Ducharme boys disappeared in the woods. Chanticleer was quiet again, but the bacon smell was real homey. She cleaned up and settled back at the table with the dead mouse.

Inside the leather satchel with her scalpels and tins of cornmeal and arsenic powder was a letter from Sam.

19

The letter was a folded piece of notepaper with her name written on the outside in the careful block letters Sam used for specimen tags.

April 22, 1927

Dear Donut,

I'm relieved to hear from Tiny that you are safe. He wouldn't tell me where you are but assures me that you have a roof over your head. I'm sending on your taxidermy tools in case an opportunity arises.

Agnes has been to see me. Your disappearance has caused her great pain and worry. It may be justified in your eyes, but you should not rest comfortably thinking she is unaffected.

Why have you run off? Agnes won't leave without you, and Donut, she's not such a bad egg.

Do come home.

Your most especial friend,
Sam

P.S. Ichabod is coming along. I'm quite pleased with the stitching.

Donut slammed the letter down on the table. Aunt Agnes had gotten to Sam. Not a bad egg. Her auntie was a downright rotten egg. And so was Sam. It'd stink real bad if they bumped heads and cracked open, the both of them. He should have convinced Aunt Agnes to give her up. Begged to be allowed to take her in—his goddaughter, too. But he wouldn't fight hard enough for her.

Donut got up and grabbed a stick of kindling. She poked the two traps along the wall. They snapped and jumped off the floor. She wasn't going to kill the mouse with the notched ear. She wasn't going to kill any more of the mice. At least they hadn't double-crossed her.

She picked up the dead mouse and held it in her palm. Growing up around Sam she'd seen her fair share of dead animals, so she wasn't going to get all busted up over it. But she wasn't going to skin it and put glass eyes in its skull, either.

She'd spent hours at Sam's learning how to use the scalpels and scrapers and needles. She liked how the rest of the world would drop away when she was working on a specimen. But now the idea of trying for a lifelike pose in something dead filled her up with sadness.

Donut crumbled a gingersnap into a pile on the counter in the shadow of the water bucket, where the notch-eared mouse might feel safer for a visit. She pulled her damp coat and boots on, went outside, and threw the dead mouse behind the woodpile for the crows. Down on the shore she looked for tracks. There was nothing but bird prints all in a jumble in the mud, like Egyptian hieroglyphics. Tonight she'd leave another apple.

Despite the clear skies it was a cold day. Her damp coat and boots drew in the chill and gave her the shivers. Walking would help warm her up, and she wasn't going to go far. Donut jumped over the muddy spots in the trail, climbed over the rotted trunk of a balsam, and hurried past the old maple. She knew she should turn around, but she didn't.

She could just sneak down the road and peek in to see how Ichabod was coming along. Sam would never spot her. He'd be too busy stitching up the seams in Ichabod's rear end like some old lady patching a sofa cushion. And Aunt Agnes wouldn't catch her. She wouldn't set foot outside in this mud.

Donut picked up her pace. She got to the rocky shore

where she and Tiny had launched the *Nehi* and didn't stop. Now that she'd decided to spy on Sam and Aunt Agnes, she was in sort of a panic to get there.

She kept to the edge of the road, listening for Ernie's Ford. When she caught sight of her house it was a fresh look, like she'd been gone for an age. The shingled roof had built up a good crop of moss, the blue trim around the windows looked worn, and the chimney with the one white brick was kicking out thick black smoke. Aunt Agnes wasn't keeping the wood furnace burning right.

Donut slipped into the yard. She had no doubt that her auntie was perched on her mother's wingback chair, click-clacking away with those knitting needles. She got past the woodpile, crouched down at the window, and peered in. She could see the back of Aunt Agnes's head above the high-backed chair. Her knitting was piled up on the side table along with her reading glasses. She was just sitting there all still and quiet. Donut turned away from the window and hurried back to the road.

Her auntie should be knitting or reading one of her books.

"Too darn bad she's worried. That's her problem."

But Donut knew that Aunt Agnes's worry was all because of her. And people didn't worry unless they cared. Donut kicked a rock into the scrub. She never should have left Chanticleer.

At Sam's, she climbed up on the bulkhead door and looked in the parlor window. He was there, crouched under the moose's belly. Ichabod was no ghost moose anymore. His dark brown fur glistened and his long, knobby legs were ready to walk right off the spruce slab. He had a distinguished beard and his gigantic antlers almost touched the ceiling. With his hunchback and droopy moose lips Ichabod wasn't elegant like a deer, but his bigness was magnificent.

Magnificent, yes, but a deep-down sadness hovered around this moose, stuck there on that spruce slab, dead. It was back in March when Sam had gotten the telegram from Maine. He'd loaded his equipment into his truck and headed north with Tiny to help with the heavy lifting. Tiny said they'd skinned the moose right there in the woods. The Great North Woods where Ichabod had grown up, lumbered around in marshes and lakes, dipped his great head into the water, gathering up delicious cress and lilies.

They'd given the meat away and left the guts for foxes and crows to eat. Probably took days and days—a feast with cawing and yapping, dancing and the fluttering of wings. There would be nothing left of Ichabod's insides now. Insects and worms would have gotten the last traces.

Donut watched Sam for a long time. Kneeling on the spruce slab, he dabbed brown paint on the seam he'd stitched to close up the hide. Sam had that look he got when she'd have to poke him with something to get his attention. She should bang open his door and whomp him over the head with one of his butterfly nets. Give him a good talking to about being an especial friend and what that really meant.

But there was no changing him, and he had offered to take her in even though it would muddle him up something terrible to have someone else living in his house. With all her heart Donut wanted to run into the parlor, give Sam a hug, and get hugged back. Because she knew he would, no matter what.

Donut pulled herself away from Sam's window and ran back to the road, keeping one step ahead of stopping, sitting down in the mud, and melting into a puddle of tears. She might just sink so deep into that mud she'd never climb back out.

She kept running until she got past her house and far enough away from Sam that she could slow down and not fall to bits.

Halfway up the hill she heard Ernie's Ford. It sputtered and groaned, coming on at top speed. He must have found the potato in the tailpipe. Donut cut off the road into the brambles. There wasn't much cover and she could hardly move, what with her coat getting snagged on the black-berry thorns—last year's canes, old and tough. She dropped to the ground just before Ernie flew by, trailing a cloud of exhaust.

Donut choked on the oily smoke. She pulled her arm

free from the thorns, heard her coat rip, wiped blood off her cheek and sucked on a deep scratch on her palm. It took a good deal of work and three more scratches to yank herself loose from the brambles and stumble back to the road.

"Ernie, go soak your head!" she yelled at the dust cloud. "You're supposed to drag me back to Aunt Agnes alive, not kill me."

Donut hoofed it up the trail, got off the road and half-way to the pond before she stopped to wipe more blood off her cheek and inspect her torn-up hands. She brushed the mud and leaves off her coat as best she could, but the scratches on her hands were tender and the brambles had caught hold of her braid and yanked it, giving her a sore scalp.

"Blast it all," she said to no one.

She made it back to the cabin—kicking rocks and stomping in the mud the whole way. She packed the stove with wood and set a pan of milk to warm up.

"Glow all you want," she said to the stovepipe.

The scratches had stopped bleeding but were sore to the touch, and the cut on her thumb from the jagged hole in the *Nehi* throbbed when she pulled on dry socks. Come August she was gonna eat every last blackberry in that good-for-nothing bramble patch.

She sat at the table with her mug of Ovaltine and the *Rand McNally World Atlas*, second edition. Breathing in the familiar scent of her atlas calmed her down some. She got out her tablet and began a sketch of the Mississippi River Delta.

But without her *Encyclopedia Britannica*, the map was flat. She couldn't pull out the M–N–O volume and read up on the history or the animals—the shipwrecks, hurricanes, and all the exotic birds and snakes that lurked in the steamy bayou there in the delta. There was no story. Like the mouse and bird skins in her mother's hope chest had no story. Stitching them up tight and gluing in glass eyes didn't let on a thing about their lives. The living, breathing notch-eared mouse was loads more interesting, what with his hankering for gingersnap crumbs, and her wondering where he slept at night and how he'd gotten that notch.

Donut closed her atlas. Tiny hadn't shown up, and it was getting dark. She carried her last apple down to the shore and set it on the flat rock. Shivering, she hurried back to the cabin. It was going to be a cold night.

She stared out the window. If only Tiny would come stomping through the door. But she knew he wouldn't. Not today. Poor Winnie. She'd seen Mr. Patoine shoot a cow once before. Tiny and her had stood by the fence, just seven or eight years old. Mr. Patoine had stroked the neck of the old cow, Lottie, talked in a way Donut had never heard, gentle and sad.

The shot was loud, made them jump. Lottie had just dropped, crumpled like she'd emptied out. It was right then that Donut understood the difference between dead and alive. Death wasn't some peaceful drifting off. It was a clap of thunder, a door slamming—Lottie, standing, swishing her tail, turned into a slack heap in an instant.

Donut sat for a long time wishing Tiny would come so she could say how sorry she was that he'd lost his beautiful Winnie.

The chill air in the cabin got her moving. She put more wood in the stove, lit the lamp, and checked on the pile of gingersnap crumbs on the counter. She changed for bed, sat back down, and ate the last of the cheese and crackers for dinner.

She blew out the lamp and gazed out at the pond. It was lit with a wide stroke of moonlight. Down by the shore the rocks were all grays and blacks, with white moon patches where there was a puddle or wet on the mud or boulders.

It was then, right then while she was watching, that the bear ambled out of the trees. He headed straight for her gift. She could see the outline of the apple. Her bear moved slowly toward it, his head down, on all fours, climbing over the rocks. Then he sat, sat on his big rump, picked up the apple in his front paws, and ate it. She watched him eat the apple while he sat there on the shore of Dog Pond with no cares in the world.

It took just a few seconds, a few bites. Donut held her breath. Didn't move. Finished, the bear gazed out across the pond. Then he hooted, kind of barked, three times, his nose up in the air. Donut and the bear were quiet then, waiting together. They waited a good long time. Then it came. Three soft barks from across the pond. Donut grinned. She couldn't help it. She grinned even though the grinning hurt the cut on her cheek. Her bear stood on all fours, lifted his head up high, and hooted back. The bear on the opposite shore answered with shorter barks, four of them. Her bear stood still for a while, then trotted, sort of galumphing like a bear does, back into the woods.

The shore was empty, then. Just shadows. Even the mice in the cabin were quiet, with a pile of gingersnap crumbs still on the counter. Donut climbed into bed, curled up into a ball under the blankets. Chanticleer was emptied out now, like the flat maps in her atlas.

20

Donut woke, coughing. Smoke. Heat. The stovepipe was alive—a deep, hot red in the dark cabin. The fire inside it rumbled, blasted up toward the roof. The whole thing like a rocket ready to blow right through the ceiling.

Fire snapped and hissed above her head. The roof was burning. She couldn't breathe. Donut pulled the blanket up over her head. To keep the smoke away. To hide. The fire crackled and roared. Get out. Get away. The blanket held her there. She kicked and tore herself free.

Coughing and choking, she stumbled out of bed, got ahold of the photo of her and her pops in the silver frame, and ran for the door. In her socks and nightgown and her mother's sleeping cap she yanked the door open and ran.

Down to the shore. She tripped and fell on the rocks, got up, and kept moving. To the water, to the rock where she'd put the apple. She stepped in the tracks of her bear, leaned over, coughed, tried to breathe, and coughed some more. Donut turned around to look.

Chanticleer was on fire. Flames and sparks shot out of the chimney pipe. The old shingled roof burned—kicked red-hot cinders high into the air, sent plumes of smoke up into the night sky. Despite all the soaking rain a few days back and the damp earth all around, Chanticleer was burning. And the noise of it was not the comfortable flickering of flames in a fireplace or a campfire. This fire howled like a wild thing in the night. Night, a time for stillness and quiet creeping.

The notch-eared mouse.

"No, no, no."

Surely he'd known when he sniffed that smoke, when he twitched those whiskers at the growing heat. He'd known like any sensible creature that he should run, leave his cozy nest, find a knothole in a tree, a crevice in a rock, far away from the fire.

Donut looked down at the photograph in the silver frame. Everything else was burning. Her *Rand McNally World Atlas*, second edition, her book bag, and the scratchy blue blankets. Her coat and boots and the orange from Mr. Hollis that she'd been saving.

She could see flames inside now, through the window. The old rickety cabin was going to burn to the ground. She'd never asked him. Marcel's cabin. She'd burned his cabin down. The old stovepipe.

Burning bits of Chanticleer were getting picked up by the wind and carried out over her head, over Dog Pond. They dropped like shooting stars, sizzled in the water. The flames lit the whole cove in a red glow. The noise of it, the cracking and bursting of wood, echoed off the hillside.

What if the whole forest began to smolder and then to burn? She had to get away. But she couldn't move. She couldn't take her eyes away from the fire. Chanticleer burning.

"Go," she said. "Move." Her voice a small thing, drowning in the roar of the fire.

In the fire's light, Donut moved along the shore. At the edge of the clearing she followed the path of her bear into the woods and up to the trail. Her stocking feet were heavy with mud. Away from the heat she began to shiver. Little moonlight made it into the thick woods. She picked her way along the trail in the dark, shuffling forward with each step, her teeth chattering with the cold. She'd escaped burning up in the fire and now she was going to freeze to death.

An enormous crash and roar filled the woods. Donut stood stock-still. The roof. The roof must have caved in. Squashed everything. The table. Tiny's chair. Her chair. All burning in a heap now.

Donut moved on, away from the noise and wildness of the fire. What was she doing, here in the woods in her night-clothes? This was just all wrong. Not her plan at all. She was cold to the bone, what with her feet in the mud and wearing just a nightgown. She gripped the silver frame in her left hand and pulled her mother's nightcap down around her ears. And she kept moving, a little faster now where the trail drew close to the pond and there were fewer trees casting black shadows.

She thought she might keel over soon. Give up and drop down on the muddy ground because of the cold and the sting of her bloody knee from falling on the rocks and from the world being such a rotten place. And then she could rest. Sleep.

Donut stopped at the old maple. She could just curl up in the hollow spot in the gnarled roots and maybe stop shivering and maybe not have such a cotton head. Her bear would come, reach down, and pick her up in his big paws, carry her, lumber along on two legs. He'd take her to her house, set her on the doorstep, and hoot a soft bark to wake her. When she woke she'd see him galumphing off to the road and back to his woods.

Donut squinted her face into a frown to stop the tears from coming at the thought of her bear rescuing her. She marched on as best she could with just socks on her feet. Socks with a few holes in them now, and so muddy they weighed her down. With each step she followed the Mississippi.

"New Orleans, Baton Rouge, Vidalia, Arkansas City, Helena, keep moving, Memphis, St. Louis, Hannibal, Keokuk, Davenport, Dubuque, La Crosse, St. Paul, Minneapolis, Bemidji. Again. Do it again. New Orleans, Baton Rouge, Vidalia . . ."

She made it to the shore opposite Chanticleer and stood on a rock and looked across Dog Pond. The flames were low to the ground now, in the hollow up against the hillside. The burning pile of what had been Marcel's camp glowed red, sending a streak of color across the water, the color of sunset.

At least the forest wasn't burning. Would Tiny see the red glow in the sky? He and his dad would be getting up soon for the first milking. It had to be close to dawn. The night had pushed on for days and days. Donut turned toward the trail. No one was coming to find her.

"St. Paul, Minneapolis, Bemidji . . ."

She stumbled over tree roots and rocks hidden in the dark, banged her shins, stubbed her toes. At the road she kept moving. She passed the field, Tiny's house. It was home she wanted. Donut stumbled down the road.

And then she was there, standing at the door to her house, her head so numb she wasn't sure whether her bear had gotten her home after all.

When she opened the door the warmth hit her, thick as soup. There was a lamp lit in the kitchen. She stood and breathed in the smell of the house, the smell of wool, of lemon polish, of books and carpets. Her legs wouldn't hold her in the warmth. She crumpled up onto the floor in a heap.

"Child, dear child," said Aunt Agnes from the doorway.

Donut felt Aunt Agnes's hand on her face, pushing back her hair.

"You'll shiver the life out of yourself, child, up, up you get."

Her auntie helped her into the parlor, set her in her mother's wingback chair. Aunt Agnes took the silver frame from Donut's grip and stood it on the side table. She pulled off the ragged, mud-caked socks. Donut didn't argue, didn't fuss. She let Aunt Agnes wrap her up in the afghan and watched as her auntie got a fire going in the fireplace.

"Child, child, where have you been?" Aunt Agnes took Donut's hands in hers. The warmth of them got her shivering more.

Donut studied her auntie's face, all teary and sad, the great black, tired circles under her eyes. "I burned it down," she said. "Right to the ground. But the notch-eared mouse, he got out, I'm sure of it."

She was crying now. Donut started blubbering, what with her auntie's warm hands and Chanticleer burned up and all the scratches and bumps she'd got on the trail on top of the others she'd already had and because her pops had died. Left her all alone and now here she was.

Aunt Agnes kneeled down on the floor in her bathrobe and put her arms around Donut, which made it worse, and Donut just gave up and cried in earnest, her whole body heaving and shaking with the weight of it all. Her auntie didn't say a word, just held on to Donut, kept the blanket wrapped up so tight she wouldn't break into a hundred bits and fly apart, which is what she'd do if Aunt Agnes let go now. There was no stopping the sobs and the hurt until it just kind of petered out on its own. Aunt Agnes pulled back just a little and used the handkerchief she always had stuffed up her sleeve to mop up Donut's face.

"Child, I don't care what you burned down. You're safe now, sitting right where I can see you."

Aunt Agnes tucked the afghan in around Donut's shoulders and sat in the chair opposite with her knitting.

"I'm going to sit right here until you fall asleep," she said.

What with the warm room and having cried herself out and her auntie sitting right there, Donut laid her head back against the chair and closed her eyes. She slept one of those deep sleeps that happen sometimes, when dreams are just colors and faces and music with no story. A faraway place.

It was Tiny and Sam who woke her up, banging on the door and charging into the house, muddy boots leaving a trail on the carpet.

"Is she here?" hollered Tiny. "Donut? Is she here?"

Donut opened her eyes, still groggy.

"Right here, safe and sound," said Aunt Agnes, getting up from her chair, tightening the belt on her bathrobe.

Tiny barged right in, stood over Donut in her chair.

"I thought you were burnt up, dead in the fire. Saw the smoke. Knew it was the camp."

"He came looking for you," said Sam in his jacket, red long johns, rubber boots. "Scared the dickens out of me when he described the pile of ashes he'd seen out at Marcel's camp."

"I burned it down," said Donut. "It was all my fault."

Tiny blew out a sigh. "But you're all right."

"Yes."

She was sad and tired and ached all over. But they were all there. All three of them, Sam, Tiny, her auntie, anchoring her to the earth like they each had ahold of one of the ribbons her mother had stitched on her white dress in the photograph of her and her pops in the silver frame.

Aunt Agnes moved closer to Donut, leaned over, and tucked the afghan in tighter around her shoulders. Tiny raised his eyebrows.

"Safe and sound," said Sam. "But you need your rest."

"And I got to get back, let my folks know you're okay." Tiny shook his head at Donut. "Ran out of the barnyard like I was off my trolley. Had to tell them you were holed up where that smoke was coming from. Ratted you out in the end, sorry."

"It's okay, Tiny. It's me that's sorry I scared you into thinking I was dead and all. For the second time."

"That's enough talk about being dead," said Aunt Agnes. "You need to rest, allow yourself to mend."

Sam patted Donut's shoulder in that way he had, all stiff and fumbling. Tiny gave her a gentle punch on the arm and they both left.

Aunt Agnes spent the rest of the day fussing over Donut. She filled the copper bath with hot water and Donut had a good scrub and got into a clean nightgown. Her slippers had burnt up along with Chanticleer, so Aunt Agnes gave her a pair of black socks from her workbasket. They were soft and warm. Probably made the men in the Soldiers' Home happy just to pull on a pair.

Aunt Agnes doctored the cuts on Donut's knees and thumb and the bramble scratches on her cheek and hands. She brushed out Donut's hair and fed her toast with butter and jam. They sat in front of the fire in the parlor, Donut sleeping, Aunt Agnes knitting a gray sock.

Every so often Donut woke and the whole night came back, full of the howling of the fire and crashing of the roof, and her auntie would look up and order her back to sleep. She did what she was told.

It was dark when Donut woke again to the click-clack

of Aunt Agnes's knitting needles filling the room. Her head wasn't stuffed with cotton anymore and she needed to stretch her legs, but she stayed still, listening. A few days ago she would have gritted her teeth at the sound. If she'd had half a chance she would have taken an ax to those knitting needles. She peeked over at her auntie. Sam just happened to be right this time around. Aunt Agnes wasn't such a bad egg after all. But now that Donut was clearheaded and rested up, there wasn't going to be any more tucking her in and monkeying around with her hair.

"I'm better, Auntie. Loads better," she said.

"About slept the day away," said Aunt Agnes.

Donut was quiet and the click-clack started up again. Her auntie had her matter-of-fact voice back. Donut didn't have to worry about getting her afghan tucked in again or her hair pushed back under her mother's sleeping cap. That worked out just fine and dandy for her, since she didn't go in for being fussed with by anybody. But it was all different now. The two of them had gone through a spring melt—all the frostiness was gone. They could get on now. It took burning down Marcel's camp to melt all that ice, but there it was.

"Auntie, why is it you send socks to the Soldiers' Home?"

Aunt Agnes stopped knitting and gazed over at Donut. "Your uncle Brodie's in the home. He's our only brother, the youngest. Until he was old enough to fend us off, your mother, Jo, and I dressed him up, treated him like a porcelain doll. He was on the Western Front in the Great War, in the trenches. Shell-shocked. Never the same. Falls apart with the noises and the great whir of the world. I knit the socks for all the men there. Jo and I visit him when we can. It's a sad place, the Soldiers' Home."

"That's awful, Auntie. I never knew I had an uncle."

The click-clack of the needles started up again.

"Pops was in the war," said Donut after a minute. "He never talked about it."

"Yes, dear, I know. We had you in Boston for the year he was overseas."

"What?" Donut sat up, pushed the afghan off, and stared at her aunt.

"You wouldn't remember, being just a year old. A holy terror when you started in walking. Jo and I had to watch you like a hawk." Aunt Agnes smiled.

"Pops never told me that. And Sam must have known. How come none of you ever said I already lived a year in Boston?"

"It was a sad time. Full of worry, and no news for weeks. And then Brodie came home, not a scratch on him, just nineteen years old but with the eyes of an old man. Not a year any of us like to talk about." Aunt Agnes smiled. "You called me Aggie."

Aggie. Donut tried to picture it, her aunties and her.

"Auntie, I'm gonna have to tell Marcel what I did to his cabin," she said.

Aunt Agnes stopped knitting and looked up. "I expect he's heard the news," she said. "The way gossip spreads in this village, he probably knew before you made it home."

"I'll have to go talk to him tomorrow."

"Yes, I just guess you will."

Donut pulled the afghan tight and gazed out the window at the moon, just rising. "I saw a bear, Auntie."

"Good lord, that shack burning down around your ears wasn't enough?"

"I left him an apple. He sat in the moonlight and ate it. After the fire, in the woods, when I was so cold and about ready to just curl up in the roots of the old maple, I thought my bear would carry me home."

"Well, then, sounds like that bear kept your spirits up. I'm beholden to the creature." Aunt Agnes smiled and went back to her knitting.

"Would you like a cup of tea?" said Donut. "I'm gonna make myself some Ovaltine."

Aunt Agnes looked up, studied Donut awhile. They studied each other.

"That would be nice," she said.

21

D onut set out for Marcel's after a late breakfast. She carried a burlap bag over her shoulder.

Tails wagging, Lafayette and Rochambeau escorted her
down the long rutted trail. Marcel was sitting on the porch
reading the *Gazette*. He didn't smile when he caught sight of
her, just set the paper down. Donut swallowed hard, and
stepped up onto the porch, the Generals leaping and jumping around.

She started right in, fast, hardly breathing. "I should
have asked you. Had no business using your camp without
your say-so. And I burned it down. Right to the ground. I'm
really sorry."

He stood, a grim look on his face. "Get over here, girl."

Donut wanted to run, but she didn't. She set her bag down on the bench and walked over to him, fists clenched, eyes squinched. Marcel reached down and picked her right up off the porch. His hands fit almost clear around her waist. Her feet dangled off the ground. She had no time to react. He leaned in and gave her a big smooch on each cheek and plunked her back down on the porch. Donut stumbled a little.

Marcel sat back down in his chair. "The Generals and I are glad you're alive."

"I'm sorry, Marcel."

He looked at her hard. Waited.

"I knew all along. Shouldn't have kept the stove so hot with that old pipe, but it was rainy and it got real cold."

"You should not have been there in the first place."

"I know, and I'll never do anything like that again."

"Words are easy. Time will tell."

Marcel stroked Lafayette's long back.

Donut dug the blackened Ovaltine can out of her sack. Tiny had brought it over when she was still sound asleep. Aunt Agnes said he'd hiked out to Dog Pond and searched the ruins of Chanticleer before morning milking.

Donut handed Marcel the can. "Here's four dollars and eighty-seven cents. I figure some of the girls at my auntie's school might be interested in starting up a weekly poker game. I'll send you all my winnings. Promise."

Marcel smiled just a little. "Your *tante* might have something to say about the poker playing. But I'll hold you to that promise. Now, we are done. No more talk of this."

Donut sat down on the porch steps and put her arms around Rochambeau. They visited for a while and she told Marcel about the *Nehi* and the bear and the notch-eared mouse.

"He's fine, your friend the mouse," said Marcel, filling his pipe. "Any creature with a brain skedaddles if he smells smoke. And you've got to consider that notch in his ear. Got out of trouble once before. An exceptionally clever mouse."

The Generals walked her back to the road. She waved goodbye and headed home.

Tiny met her hiking up the hill.

"Thanks for finding my money."

"That was all that was left. How'd it go with Marcel?"

"Glad it's over. He was a peach in the end," said Donut.

Tiny wasn't throwing rocks. That's how she knew.

"Winnie's gone, isn't she?"

Tiny stopped walking and looked at his boots. "My dad put her down two days ago."

Donut grabbed his big hand and gave it a squeeze. He shook his head. "That cow just got ahold of me. Don't know why."

They started walking again. Donut didn't know how she was going to tell him. Tell him she was leaving.

"Tiny," she said.

He gave her a punch on the arm. "I know. Saw you with your auntie the other night. You're going, aren't you?"

"You're my best friend," said Donut, trying to find the words. "I'll miss you something awful, and I'm sorry I'm leaving now, with Winnie gone."

"Won't be the same without you," said Tiny. He leaned over and picked up a rock and stuffed it in his pocket. "Hey, I gotta get home—chores."

"See you tomorrow."

"Yeah."

She stood watching Tiny hike up Slapp Hill Road and let the tears drip down her cheeks for a while.

"Staying or going. It stinks both ways," she said to herself. Donut wiped her face with her coat sleeve and started walking home.

Aunt Agnes was in the kitchen chopping turnips. Turnips.

"How was your visit?"

"We worked it out." Donut sat at the table and fidgeted with the pepper shaker. "Auntie, I don't want to go."

Aunt Agnes came over and sat down. "I know. But there's just no other way. I have to get back. Already I've been away too long."

"It's not the same now, my not wanting to go. I'm kind of scared of Boston and the school and all of it being different, but a little excited, too. It's losing Sam and Tiny. The whole village."

Aunt Agnes nodded. They sat quietly for a while at the table.

"I'll be leaving Pops, too. He's here, everywhere."

Donut picked at the scab on her thumb. The *Nehi* was still here, too, sitting quietly at the bottom of Dog Pond. She'd never get her boat back. She'd never get her village back, either, not like it was before, because she wasn't going to get her pops back. Aunt Agnes reached out and took ahold of both of her hands. "It's hard to lose people."

Her auntie got up and started in chopping again. She didn't try to sugarcoat any of it. She was like that—honest. Donut figured if she was going to let someone take charge of her again, Aunt Agnes wasn't such a bad choice.

"You know, Auntie, I don't like turnips. Not one bit."

"Well, why on earth didn't you tell me that before? I've been feeding you turnips for weeks." And then Aunt Agnes started in laughing—the very first time Donut had heard her laugh.

"I don't like oatmeal much, either."

Aunt Agnes laughed harder. Donut grinned at her auntie and her auntie grinned back with the all-out truthfulness of a dog's tail wagging. Donut knew right then that it was going to be okay.

The night before she and Aunt Agnes were getting on the train to Boston, Donut hiked down the hill to Sam's.

Wally and Pete appeared, tearing up the hill toward her.

"Hey, boys," she said.

"Got something for you," said Wally. He handed her a slingshot.

"Applewood," said Pete.

"It's a beauty," said Donut.

She fingered the smooth wood, perfectly balanced with a slice of rubber inner tube threaded through holes drilled in the ends.

"Made it special for you to have in the city," said Wally. "For protection, what with all the shootouts and car chases."

"I think that's just in the moving pictures," said Donut, laughing. "But it should come in handy when I wanna stir things up in my aunties' school."

They grinned.

"Good luck," said Wally.

"Yeah, good luck," said Pete.

"Thanks, and for the bacon and eggs, too."

The boys turned and raced down the hill.

As Donut neared Sam's house she heard a ruckus in the dooryard. In the fading light Marcel and Tiny were busy strapping down an enormous wooden crate in the bed of Sam's truck.

"That should hold," said Tiny.

"Guess you know your onions," said Marcel, laughing.

Tiny led Donut over to the side of the house. A rough

opening the size of a barn door was cut right out of the parlor wall. A wooden ramp ran up to the opening.

"Thought we'd bring the whole house down," he said. "Slid the crate with old Ichabod inside right down the ramp."

A huge pile of what used to be part of Sam's house sat off to the side. Donut leaned down and picked up a scrap of the parlor wallpaper—all violets and roses.

"Says he's gonna have a proper door installed so he won't have any troubles in the future."

While Tiny checked the crate with Marcel, Donut went into Sam's house through the front door. She stood in the mudroom surrounded by his flock. Her red-winged blackbird was on the top shelf next to Arthur. She couldn't have left it on her workbench, just the skin, emptied out. In between packing and goodbyes, she'd worked with Sam to build an armature, perch her blackbird on a bulrush, wings spread ready to leap into the air and fly.

"You've got a new flock now," she whispered to the blackbird. "Take care of them all, Arthur."

They played poker until late into the night. Donut had special permission from Aunt Agnes as long as Tiny walked her home. Her auntie didn't trust the dark now that she'd learned there were bears roaming around. She'd loaned Donut a poker stake of fifty cents since she'd given all her money to Marcel.

Tiny and Donut were quiet on the walk back. At the door he gave her a sock on the arm.

"You sure about this? We could come up with another plan."

"I don't want to go to Boston," said Donut, looking up at Tiny. "I want everything to be the way it was before. But I'll be all right with my aunties. And you know I'll be back to stay with Sam for all of July."

Tiny nodded.

"Look out for him 'til then," said Donut.

"Yeah."

Donut reached into her coat pocket and pulled out the seashell that had always sat on her windowsill in her room. She put it in his hand.

"This is for you, Tiny. Anytime you want, you can listen to the ocean. Pops found it ages ago."

Tiny studied the shell and put it against his ear. He got a faraway look on his face. "I can hear it. Waves."

"Aunt Agnes said you should come visit. We can go to a real beach and a baseball game, too. At Fenway Park."

"I'm gonna miss you something terrible," said Tiny.

"Me, too," said Donut.

They stood there in the doorway for a good while. Tiny fingered the shell in his right hand. Donut got up on her tiptoes and gave him a kiss on the cheek, backed off, and grabbed for the doorknob.

She turned and hurried into the house.

Marcel drove them to the train station the next morning with all their bags and boxes, including Donut's mother's hope chest. Donut had given Sam all her practice specimens except one. The very last mouse she'd stitched up was carefully wrapped in red flannel at the bottom of her mother's chest. It was the closest she'd gotten to alive—the glass eyes lined up so perfectly, that little mouse was ready to scamper back into its nest somewhere in the kitchen cupboards.

Mrs. Lamphere had made up a lunch for them along with a sack of gingersnaps. Doris had given Donut the latest issue of *True Confessions* to read on the train.

"You've just got to write me long letters. Tell me all about the city."

"I will. I promise," said Donut.

Sam had gone ahead in his truck. When they'd said their goodbyes to Marcel, Agnes and Donut joined Sam on the platform.

"Hey, Sam. Is Ichabod all settled in?" said Donut.

"Built the crate double strong. But I'm glad to have you as an escort for the old fellow, at least until he changes trains in Boston. House feels empty without him, and it was a little cold this morning with the breeze blowing in."

She put her arms around him and breathed in the sweet smell of his pipe tobacco.

"I'm gonna miss you," he said, patting her shoulder. "But you'll be back this summer."

"Bye, Sam," said Donut, her voice muffled in his jacket. "You're a swell godfather."

She stepped back a few steps and he scrubbed at his hair and smiled.

"Thank you," said Aunt Agnes. "For looking out for our girl here."

They settled into their seats on the train. For a long while, Donut sat very still, tears dripping off her chin. Her auntie patted her knee and gave her a handkerchief.

It was a long trip, with lots of stops and starts. Aunt Agnes's knitting needles kept up a steady click-clack. Donut studied the towns along their route in her brand-new *Rand McNally World Atlas*, third edition. She smiled at the thought of Ichabod standing in the dark crate in the baggage car at the end of the train.

Donut laid her head against the window, closed her eyes, and whispered, "Cobden, Hardwick, Walden, Danville, Saint Johnsbury, Wells River, Lakeport, Concord, Manchester, Nashua, Lowell, Boston. Got it."

ACKNOWLEDGMENTS

I am grateful to my Vermont students and friends for deepening my understanding of life in the Northeast Kingdom of Vermont: Betty and Bill Corrow, Dean Stratton and his unforgettable mom, Mary, Jan Howard, Laurie Heath, Joe Williams, Levi Chase, Kory and Kolin Barclay, Braiden and Garrett Mayo and Caitlyn Frost. The Vermont State Library and The Vermont Historical Society provided invaluable research materials. Thanks to the librarians and staff.

Vermont College of Fine Arts is an extraordinary place to learn and grow as a writer. Thank you to the entire VCFA community and especially my graduating class, the Sweet Dreamers and my advisors—Julie Larios, Sarah Ellis, Leda Schubert and Rita Williams Garcia. Many thanks to Shelley Tanaka, Dana Walrath, Sarah Aronson, Anne Cardinal, Margaret Bechard, Sharon Darrow and Alan Cumyn for valuable feedback and to Elizabeth Law for telling me to finish the book. My retreat buddies, Jessica Dils and Mima Tipper, you are wonderful readers and steady friends. Tod Olson, Laura McCaffrey and Leda

Schubert—our dinners together and friendship keep me plugging along. Hugs to my sister, Erica, and my whole family. And thanks to Corina and K.P.

Bridget and Tomás, my cuñados, you've been there throughout, reading early and later drafts. Bridget, you are my especial friend who listens to my stories and helps me get over the bumps in the road on our walks in the woods.

Susan Hawk, you are brilliant, supportive and utterly reliable. I am lucky to have you as my agent. Many thanks to my editors, Anna Roberto and Jean Feiwel, who helped get this story over the finish line, to Karl James Mountford for a gorgeous cover, and the whole team at Feiwel and Friends.

Georg Kalmar—you listened to me read aloud every word as I moved through many, many drafts helping me to hear and tell this story. Thank you for your love and support and patience. Abrazos.

Thank you for reading this
Feiwel and Friends book.

The friends who made

A
STITCH
IN TIME

possible are:

Jean Feiwel, Publisher

Liz Szabla, Associate Publisher

Rich Deas, Senior Creative Director

Holly West, Editor

Anna Roberto, Editor

Christine Barcellona, Editor

Kat Brzozowski, Editor

Alexei Esikoff, Senior Managing Editor

Raymond Ernesto Colón, Senior Production Manager

Anna Poon, Assistant Editor

Emily Settle, Assistant Editor

Rebecca Syracuse, Associate Designer

Ilana Worrell, Production Editor

Follow us on Facebook or visit us online at mackids.com.
Our books are friends for life.